GNO

GIRLS NIGHT OUT

JENNIFER SEGALLA

This book is dedicated to my three loves,
Nadia, Isabella and Julianna.
Love makes everything possible.

STAGES

Great Expectations   1

Natalia   13

Bekka   15

Bekka   19

   (Tuesday)

Liv   24

Bekka   27

   (Wednesday)

Nat   29

   (Wednesday)

Bekka   32

   Ted & Sympathy (Thursday!)

Nat   37

   Dirty Stay Out (Thursday)

Liv   38

Nat   43

   How Sweet It Is (TGIF)

Bekka   46

Friyay!   48

Natalia   50

   Diamonds in The Rough

Liv   52

   Big Love (Saturday)

Girls Just Wanna Have Fun!   57

The Hotel   87

"Eat, Shop & Be Millionaires"   105

Manic Monday   130

Whatever After   146

Epilogue   150

   Olivia (4 weeks later)

Acknowledgements   153

GREAT EXPECTATIONS

Olivia sat heavily in the chair. She makes brief eye contact with her therapist as her puffy eyes well up.

"When you're ready please begin," Dr. Robbins says as she places a fresh box of tissues on the end table.

Liv lets out a big exhale. "I'm exhausted."

"Take your time, dear. Whenever you're ready."

"Jack is cheating on me!" Liv blurts out as she reaches for a tissue and starts balling.

"Are you sure?"

"Yes, yes I'm sure!" Liv screams.

"I'm sorry, I didn't mean to-- I am sorry to hear this. I know you've had your suspicions."

Liv slides out of the chair and drifts across the room to the window. "It's all my fault! I blame it on my fortuitous encounter. It's a curse as much as a blessing! He leads a charmed life, that bastard!" Liv roars as she looks out and witnesses the rush hour traffic.

"He has been different lately. I don't know who he is. Am I an enabler?" Liv sobs.

"You know that's not true, Liv. You're upset. You feel disrespected, taken for granted. It's normal."

"I'm angry. I feel betrayed! I'm not sure how to process it." With her arms folded under her chest, Liv pivots away from the window, walks softly back to the chair and sits.

"Well Liv, let's work on breaking it down. After all, this is our third session and I don't have a full perspective on your marriage, and your life. I need more so I can help you find the silver lining. You've made some significant decisions over the past several months. Smart selfless decisions that took you on a new journey. You brought hope and positive things into the lives of the people you love and others. Don't let it all fall to pieces. You stated last week that Jack was notorious for being a killjoy. Don't allow that to be the case."

"I know. I am being a mental filter. It's difficult to be emotionally buoyant at the moment."

"It's normal, Liv."

"How does one recover from this? The pain is piercing." Liv shrieks.

"I believe we can make progress if we look at the days preceding your girl's night out. It will give me a better understanding of how much has changed. The answers will come. Sometimes one needs to hear themselves talk about it. It will help break down bad behavior and dynamics that lead up to the current state of your life and marriage. I promise you will find the silver lining."

Liv sits there continuing to listen quietly, taking it all in.

"You sought therapy for a reason, Liv. It may be because you feel you've lost control. It's important to focus on your struggles and find healthy options on how to cope without jumping the gun and heading straight for divorce. Think about it and make some notes before our next session. Consider the things that could have been red flags, but were ignored. In the meantime, Liv, look at the glass half full, because it is."

"Ok, I will," Liv responds softly, feeling numb, she grabs her coat and exits the building. The bitter cold morning air hits her in the face as she flags a taxi and heads to her office.

An hour later, Liv sits at a lease signing in her plush upper west side conference room, perpetually clicking her pen as she observes her clients. A couple in their mid-thirties are reviewing lease documents she neatly placed in front of them. Liv starts daydreaming. She reflects back to three decades ago to her youthful mind, and how it convinced her money was the answer to everything.

Olivia Grey Sardi didn't have a charmed childhood with oodles of money, but she did have a curious mind. She observed everything, especially people who had money. At sixteen, her beat up Buick Skylark puttered down smoothly paved roads, to the homes of the uber-wealthy, where she observed the magnificence of it all. Sprawling houses with hedges perfectly pruned like a piece of a puzzle. The artfully designed landscape and the iron gates created the illusion of privacy. It was magazine worthy and left Liv to wonder what magical place stood beyond them.

Olivia's car, which was notorious for moving slowly even when she gunned the gas pedal, gave her the stealth-like advantage of getting a glimpse through the iron gates. It projected beyond the curved driveway lined with expensive automobiles, to glass front doors with regal doorknobs, ending at the sparkly chandelier hanging in the entryway. It took her breath away. It was paradise. It was better than she could have imagined! A peephole into the lavish lifestyles of the rich. It looked pretty good and excited her! Some homes had names to match their architectural personality. They all said "MONEY"! Look what it can buy you.

It took Liv until her late twenties to change her opinion about money. By that time in her life, she heard enough stories about friends, friends of friends, and family members who had to make radical lifestyle changes. Some were spendthrifts, made poor business decisions, gambled away their inheritance or went through a so-called "War of the Roses" divorce.

Liv did realize that money does, in fact, buy you freedom but if you took your eye off the ball it could be the root of all evil. A worthless necessity that stirs up greed and power.

In Olivia's mind, there was only one thing that made the world go 'round and that was love! L, O, V, E! Well, at least in her world! That intense feeling you have for someone or something, or that someone has for you.

The couple that sat across from Olivia seem unaffected by the negative things money could stir up. Her clients, Dara and James Vanderwood, were unusually normal. It was obvious that their adoration for one another was mutual. Olivia hadn't seen either of them without a smile in the forty-eight hours since she met them. James smiled as he passed the pen to his beautiful naturally born Swedish wife to sign the lease to their stunning apartment on Central Park South.

Olivia wants to cherish this moment almost as much as they do! Not one thing about them disappoints her. They're classy, educated and both from prominent families. They were blessed with a fortunate upbringing, attended private schools, Ivy league colleges and spent summers in Nantucket. They seem to have the choice to do what they want, not what they had to. Everything Olivia has ever dreamed of.

She struggled to stay in the moment. The brief thought of what she was personally facing in her marriage, nonetheless her uncharmed childhood, going to school, working three jobs, and helping her mother raise her siblings made her stir in her chair. She uncrossed her legs as she witnessed a pigeon landing on the window ledge, then she smiled as she returned her attention to her clients.

"Olivia, Dara's mother, our guarantor, is running thirty minutes late. Traffic is impossible due to an accident. She's coming from Connecticut," mentioned James.

"No worries at all. It's tough traveling into the city especially on Fridays. Plus, the holiday season is approaching," Olivia replies.

"We're going to take a short break and grab a coffee. Would you like anything?" James asks.

"No, but thank you. Please go ahead. There's a great place right across the street. Let's meet back here in thirty."

"Perfect!" chirps James.

Olivia stands up as James helps Dara with her coat, then grabs her hand and exits through the glass door sweeping her into the elevator. Olivia closes the door and travels to the window. She stares at the pigeon until her eyes are drawn downward to the people bustling down the street. She notices James and Dara at the corner. They kiss. Olivia follows them with her eyes as they cross the street. They disappear into the coffee shop. Olivia wonders if Dara knew her future arrived the day she met James. Olivia starts to reflect back to the day her future arrived.

It's all very vivid in her mind. The flickering headlights, car fumes, the banging sound, scent of puke and claustrophobia.

10 Months Ago...
Fifty Shades of Chaos

Olivia is passed out on the sofa. DING. Her phone goes off. She opens one eye, peeks at her phone to see the text message, then returns to dreamland.

After a while, the sound of her mother's ringtone wakes her. As she attempts to sit up, her dense textbook slides off her thighs, and hits the floor.

"Hi Mom," she squeaks out as she glances at her watch.

"Hi, Liv. What's going on?"

"Can I call you back in a few minutes?"

"Of course, darling. Is everything ok? You sound weird. I heard a loud noise."

"Nothing Mom, I'm fine. My book fell off the couch. I dozed off. I'll call you back in five minutes when I'm in the car, bye!"

Olivia places the book on the counter, grabs her purse and heads out the door. She drives hastily to pick up her daughters at school. As she idles at the traffic light, her phone buzzes. "Hi, Nikki!"

"Hi, Mom."

"I'm on my way. Are you with your sisters?"

"Yes Mom, we're all together."

"See you in a few."

"Bye Mama."

"Bye love."

The revving engine of a Mustang idling nearby grabs her attention as she calls her mother.

"Hi Mom, how are you feeling?"

"I'm feeling better Liv, thank you. Not sure how I got this stomach flu but I'm glad it's over. Must have been the change in the weather. Are you picking up my beautiful granddaughters?"

"Yes, I am."

"How was class today?"

"Good, it was really good. I'm enjoying it. The teachers are wonderful. They tell interesting stories. Some are really funny. A few more classes to go until I take the exam."

"Glad to hear it dear."

Giggling, Liv replies "After class this morning, I planned on studying but as soon as I put my head in my book, I fell asleep."

"Well, you must be exhausted. I always say, listen to what your body is telling you. It's okay to take breaks, Liv and get the rest you need."

"I know, I know Mom. I just arrived at the school. I have to go. I'll give you a call tomorrow when I have more time to chat. I'm glad you're feeling better. Love you!"

"Love you too, Liv. Kiss the girls for me. Bye honey."

Olivia slowly pulls up to the curb, as she spots the girls. She unlocks the doors. The passenger door flies open. Nikki and Bea start fighting instantly over the front seat. Bea yanks at Nikki's thick long ponytail. Nikki yells "stop" and pinches Bea's arm. Juliet ignores her sisters and says "Hey Mom," as she slides into the back seat and rests her long blonde mane on the headrest.

"Really, girls? You're fighting over the front seat. Aren't you tired from school? We'll be home in less than ten minutes. How about you both sit in the back!" Olivia shouts.

"Really! The two of you need to grow up. You're two big babies!" blurts Juliet. Nikki and Bea climb into the back seat unresponsive.

"How was school, girls?"

"GOOD!" they all respond.

"I need you to sign my field trip paper, mom."

"Ok Juliet, I will."

"I need fifteen dollars for gym pants, and I need you to sign my field trip paper," says Bea.

"Mom, I got a 92 on my math test," declares Nikki. "I have another test tomorrow and Friday. They love to overload us in eighth grade."

"Yes, they give a lot of homework compared to when I was in school. Wait 'til you get to high school."

"Juliet, where's your field trip?"

"Coney Island, Mom. It was supposed to be the Central Park Zoo, but our teacher took a vote and the majority of the 6th graders wanted to ride the cyclone. So, we're going next Tuesday."

"That's cool."

"How about you, Bea?

"My class is going to the boring zoo. This is the only time I wish I was in the same class as Juliet. You know how much I love that rollercoaster."

"Don't worry, Daddy and I will take you in the Spring, when the weather is warmer," Liv promises as she pulls into the driveway.

WOOF. WOOF.

"I hear the dogs!" giggles Nikki.

"I wish I could take them to school."

"Well Nikki, no one would learn a thing if dogs were allowed in schools."

"I guess, but we would learn about the dogs," Nikki states as they pile out of the car.

"That's true. Everyone wash up, and grab a snack."

"Nikki, please let the dogs out in the yard before you start your homework."

"Ok, Mom. "

"I'm going to start preparing dinner girls."

"What are we having Mom?" asks Juliet.

"Meatloaf and mashed potatoes!"

"Yay!" says Bea.

Olivia is in the zone chopping onions and listening to Pandora until she overhears the girls screaming from the living room. She puts down her knife on the chopping block and walks over to see what's going on. Juliette is pushing Bea. They're playing tug of war with a pencil.

"Girls, girls! Here we go again. Just get another pencil! You're fighting over nonsense, again! And Nikki, don't forget you have dance class today."

"I know, mom."

"Do you have a lot of homework?"

DING-DONG.

"Someone get the door please."

"Woof, woof," the dogs are barking from the backyard.

"Mom, it's UPS. They need you to sign," Juliette yells from the hallway.

"I'll be right there."

Olivia signs for the packages and carries them into the kitchen. Daisy is chasing Tito around the house with a sock in her mouth.

"Who let the dogs in when I said to leave them out?"

"Me, mom. I wanted to play with them," Nikki replies.

"You have to leave for dance class in forty-five minutes so do your homework. Please put the dogs in the crate. I'm going to get the laundry. I'll be right back."

"Mom, can I open the boxes from Amazon?" asks Nikki.

"No, Nikki, just do your homework!" Liv snaps.

Liv enters the laundry room and a moment later she hears Juliet calling her.

"Mom, Mom!".

"Yes, what is it?"

"Tito threw up!"

"Ok!"

"I think he ate one of the pencils, Mom."

"Give me a minute, sweetie. I'll be right there."

Liv carries the laundry basket into the living room.

"Yuk! It smells so bad."

"I'll clean it up mom, don't worry."

"Ok thanks, Jules.

Liv puts the meatloaf in the oven, sets the timer and starts folding the laundry. "Hey Bea, please set the table for dinner when you're done with homework."

"Ok, mom. I'm almost done."

"Any tests tomorrow sweetie?"

"No, but I have two on Friday. It's too much!"

Liv chuckles at Bea's animated response.

"Yes, it seems it's all or nothing but maybe you won't get homework over the weekend."

"Yeah, right! My teachers would have to be absent for that to happen," states Bea.

"Mom I'm leaving now for dance," yells Nikki.

"Ok, bye sweetie. Text me when you're there. Come straight home afterward for dinner."

"Ok, mom."

Liv texts Jack to let him know dinner will be ready in an hour.

Cool! he replies

On my way home. Busy day today, no time for lunch. I'm famished.

A few hours later, Liv is exhausted as she finishes unloading the dishwasher. She turns to   Jack. He is sprawled across the couch watching Law & Order.

"Jack, I'm wiped out. I'm going to head upstairs and try to find something on Netflix."

"Ok, I'm tired myself. This is the first time I sat down all day."

"I know the feeling, Jack."

"What are the girls doing?"

"They're all in Nikki's room watching a movie."

"Okay."

As Liv heads up the stairs, she hears the girls giggling and checks in on them.

"What are you watching, girls?"

"Mean Girls!" says Bea.

Liv chuckles.

"You never get sick of that movie. You've seen it a dozen times."

"It's funny mom. Come watch it with us" says Nikki.

"If mommy wasn't so tired, she would. I'm going to bed. Please don't go to sleep too late. It's almost 9:30."

"Ok," they all respond.

"Good night. Love you girls."

Liv smiles as she heads to her bedroom feeling blessed. Motherhood is a tough job that requires one to wear many hats. A job she knows is not cut out for everyone.

Liv's childhood was turbulent. It matured her and made her independent at a very young age. As she grew older, she became a woman with goals. An overachiever. She welcomed diversity and challenges. There was no doubt she was a moxie girl, and an opportunist.

At age eleven, Liv's father ran off with his secretary leaving her, two siblings, and her mother broken-hearted and penniless. She, being the eldest, instantaneously took on the role of handling household chores, cooking, and taking care of her sisters while her mother was at work.

As the years passed, being domesticated was second nature for Liv. Unbeknownst to her, it prematurely prepared her for motherhood, and the super mom she is to her three daughters. When she and Jack were expecting their first child, Liv was confident and excited, unlike most women who become anxious.

Luckily, during the pregnancy, Jack's hairdressing career took off and Liv was blessed with not having to face the awful emotional and financial struggles her mother had. She was a stay at home mom for years with a part-time nanny when the twins were born. Jack hustled and worked six days a week to grow his business. Thankfully today, he has two salons in New York City.

Liv washes up and crawls into bed. She places her real estate exam book in front of her. Halfway through the second chapter review, she starts daydreaming about her new career and how much it excites her. She misses being out in the workforce.

It has been over a decade and a lot has changed for women. She knows it will give her the independence and freedom she's been longing for. I'll meet people, tour beautiful properties, gain knowledge of the industry and work in Manhattan again, yay! I've always loved the energy of that city since the day I moved there in my twenties.

DING! Suddenly, her thoughts were interrupted by her phone. As she read a group text from Natalia & Rebekka, her two best friends, a smile spread across her face.

Hey ladies, let's go out this Saturday night!!! It's long overdue. Need some fun with my two favorite gal pals. Let me know if you're in or out. I can come to Brooklyn.

Immediately, Liv feels excited and responds- *I'm in!*

A few minutes later, Bekka responds- *sounds fun! Just need to check with Larry and see if he can be with the kids. Will text you tomorrow. Looking forward to it! Good night.*

Liv thought, well this is exciting and long overdue. Something to look forward to. Her mind starts to race. What will I wear? A dress with boots or platforms? Liv checks her weather app to help decide. Then she jumps out of bed, places her book on the nightstand and heads straight to her closet and starts sifting through it.

NATALIA

Natalia Kozlov leans on her kitchen counter smiling as she places her phone down after texting with Bekka and Liv. She is long legged at 5'9" even without a pair of stilettos. A naturally blond Russian beauty recently divorced and returned to live in New York City, the most energetic city in the world. Natalia, aka Nat, is on a mission to find Mr. Right and never look back on the decade-long marriage to Dean. He was a drug addict, gambler, cheater and narcissist. He became more and more emotionally abusive over the years.

The day Natalia returned home from work to their Brooklyn apartment to find it unoccupied by Dean and all his belongings was the day the tie was severed. As the hours passed, she felt more and more relief that he was out of her life. She rapidly filed for divorce and within two weeks she moved into a small one bedroom walk up on the upper east side. The transition was seamless for her. Nat was completely sucked into a vortex of total adventure and excitement from the very first day she returned to her beloved city. The thought of her new life and new everything resulted in a few sleepless nights the first week.

By week two, she was well into the groove of things. She was out every night at a trendy restaurant or night club with colleagues. By the third week, she had a date lined up. The idea of a date in twelve years to someone other than Dean gave her butterflies in her stomach. After a few months, he was a faded memory and it felt as if she never left Manhattan. She knew the city like the back of her hand since abruptly moving there with her mother and sister following a family tragedy in Russia when she was in her early teens.

It was the mid-nineties in Azov, Russia following a very long work-day. Her father had fallen asleep at the wheel, drove off a cliff and died instantly. Natalia was eleven years old at the time. She, her mother, and seven-year-old sister Elani were beyond devastated. A month following poppy's death, their mother showed up at school, dismissed them early and took them home. She sat them down on the shabby couch in the living room and announced they were moving to the US at the end of the month.

"We're going to live with Aunt Esther in Manhattan until we can manage on our own" she announced with tears in her eyes. We don't have any family left here and I don't know how to go on without your father. Auntie E already has a job lined up for me in New York. I will be working as a nanny for a nice family on Park Avenue. She enrolled the two of you in a good public school. I think it will be good for all of us. We will be with the only family we have left and if it doesn't work out, we can always come back here."

Natalia and Elani sat speechless for a few minutes. Then Elani spoke, "Ok Mama as long as the three of us are together."

"Okay, Mama but I'm scared," Nat cried out in a trembling voice.

"I am scared too. We will be fine, I promise. Your father would want this for us. At the moment, this is our only option to survive and I believe it's a very good one. Trust me when you're a mother you will understand what motherly instincts mean and mine are telling me to go to New York."

Natalia and Elani balled their eyes out on the sofa until they were fast asleep. Two weeks later, they boarded a plane to the US feeling sad and broken-hearted without papa as they bid Russia goodbye.

BEKKA

"Hmm, a girl's night out is just what I need," thinks Bekka aloud, as she reads Nat's text.

Bekka yawns, feeling exhausted from her long workday. It was a typical Monday, but the day ended perfectly with a dose of Ted. She smiles as she rewinds the events of her day.

Her throat felt a bit sore after making thirtysomething phone calls for the upcoming holiday alumni gala. Ted, her boss, spent the day in meetings. She hadn't seen him since the morning in the company kitchen filling his coffee cup. And she wasn't expecting to. Just as she was ready to leave her office, he summoned her. She entered his office with her coat and satchel over her arm. He gave her a visual massage, from his office chair as she walked from the doorway to the front of his desk.

"How was your day?" he asks.

"Productive! Lots of phone calls and emails. Making good progress with the gala."

"Yours?" she asks, taking a seat.

"Draining. One meeting after another. Thinking of you dear, was my savior."

"Hmm, I can imagine," Bekka replies.

"Is it possible you can stay a while, beautiful? I would like to spend some time together. Besides, I couldn't wait till our weekly lunch date to see you" he says softly as employees scuffle past his office door yelling, "good night Ted."

"Yes, I can stay a while," Bekka whispers back with a smile.

Once the office is vacant, Ted stands up, saunters across the room, closes the door and locks it. He turns and stares at Bekka smiling.

"I've been dreaming of this moment all day" he expresses as he heads towards his office coat closet. He withdraws two rocks glasses, and a bottle of Johnny Walker from the shelf.

"Drink?"

"Sure, but only one," she says in a jovial tone.

He fills the glasses and hands one to Bekka.

"To us" he toasts.

"To us" Bekka repeats.

Ted walks to the settee, takes a seat and crosses his legs. He holds his drink and gazes across at Bekka.

"It's been a long stressful day," he states.

"I can imagine," Bekka replies, placing her glass on the desk. She walks over to the window to admire the colossal view of the Verrazano bridge. She feels the heat of Ted's eyes on her. This is their norm, their foreplay.

Bekka puts her hands on her hips, clenches the sides of her skirt and slowly hikes it up to expose her garters.

Ted is quiet as he stares from the top of her red chestnut mane right down to her stiletto heels.

"Jesus," he groans.

She swivels on her heels, starts unbuttoning her blouse revealing just enough cleavage and lace to make Ted's face turn rosy with excitement.

He places his glass on the end table, slowly un-crosses his legs and sinks down into the sofa, expressing a pleasurable groan.

She walks over to him and kneels down. He unzips his fly exposing his erection as he stares at her cleavage.

Instantaneously, her thoughts are interrupted by the sound of Chad & Addy thumping down the stairs. Bekka returns to reality, and places dinner on the table.

"Hey Mom, when will Dad be home?" asks Chad.

"What are we having for dinner Mom?" asks Addy.

"Have a seat. I made mac and cheese and stir fry broccoli. Your favorite!"

"Yum!" Addy responds.

"Daddy won't be home until after ten and you'll be in bed way before."

"Can we stay up and wait for him, Mom?"

"No, it will be too late."

"He works too much," Addy cries out.

"Yeah, really. He hasn't had dinner with us since last week" states Chad.

"I know, I know. He has been working a lot. We all miss him, but you can't stay up that late. You have a Spanish test tomorrow, Chad. A goodnight sleep and a healthy breakfast will help you stay focused."

"Okay, Mom," Chad moans.

"You need all the help you can get," Addy says as she yawns.

"Shut up! You think you know it all! You're only twelve!"

"You mean we're twelve. I am smarter! My grades prove it. Females are smarter than males right from birth. Don't ever forget it!"

"Enough," says Bekka giggling.

"No fighting at the table. Just eat!"

After dinner, Bekka watches TV with her kids, then puts them to bed at nine. She returns to the couch and turns on an episode of Homeland. Fifteen minutes later she's fast asleep.

BEKKA

(Tuesday)

The following day, Bekka was in the weeds planning the gala that she'd forgotten her weekly lunch date with Ted, until he sent her a text.

Happy Tuesday! Guess who's taking you to lunch today! Meet you in the parking lot at noon.

Bekka was happy to have an excuse to take a break and leave the office. Plus, she was always excited to be with Ted. He was handsome, charismatic, and genuinely cared about her. She loved the connection they had.

She met Ted in the parking lot and immediately they started flirting with each other as they headed towards their cars. The second Ted removed his finger from Bekka's exposed thigh they heard the sound of a horn and then-- "Darling I'm here! Over here!" waved Shelly, his wife, from the window of her Cadillac Escalade idling at the opposite end of the parking lot.

"Ted, I'm here to take you to lunch. We're going to your favorite place, Nuno's!"

"Fuck," Ted mumbled under his breath as he cocked his neck in her direction.

Bekka's shoulders sink with disappointment as she musters up a smile and waves a quick hello to Shelly.

"Hello dear, why don't you join us?" Shelly asks.

"Oh, no. I have some errands to run, but thank you anyway" responds Bekka.

"But a girl's gotta eat, so join us. I insist!"

Ted chimes in, "Yeah. Join us. It would be nice" grabbing Bekka tightly by the arm and moving her in the direction of the SUV.

Bekka shot Ted an angry look, hesitated for a moment and then jumped into the car. The next forty-five minutes grew more and more dreadful for Bekka. She never felt more uncomfortable in her life. She sat directly across from Ted and his Irish wife of twenty-four years. She had enough of them being all kissy-kissy. They were behaving like teenagers and she lost her appetite watching them. They shared a few laughs but Bekka grew more and more angry. Angry at herself for not going with her gut and saying no! It brought out the jealousy in her. It turned her day upside down.

She cried in the ladies' room when she returned to the office and could not concentrate on the rest of her day's workload. She had strong feelings for Ted. She loved him and the guilt of their almost two-year affair overwhelmed her. Bekka remained in her office the rest of the day feeling numb from today's emotional grenade. As soon as the clock hit five o'clock, she exited the building hastily to avoid Ted.

She checked in with Chad & Addy on her way home to see what they were up to. Tonight, was pizza night at Nana's house which Bekka had forgotten. Bekka was relieved she didn't have to cook. Larry was working late again so she picked up some sushi for herself and headed straight home. As soon as she walked in the door an excited Chad called her.

"Hi, Mom! Why don't you stop by Nana's? We're just starting to make the pizza and you can help."

"Aww honey thank you, but I had a long day. I just got home and I'm going to relax."

"Okay, Mom. Nana said she'll drive us home around eight."

"Sounds good."

"I'll bring some pizza home for you" Addy yelled in the background.

Bekka laughs. "I love you both. Have fun and I'll see you later!"

Bekka spends time catching up on laundry and then takes a bubble bath enjoying the peacefulness of the house. Shortly after, Chad and Addy arrive home and talk about their fun evening with Nana. Bekka laughs as she takes a bite of the pizza and compliments how good it is.

Afterwards, she tucks Chad & Addy in bed and heads to the sofa with her laptop. Her heart sinks as she reads an email from Ted. She thought to avoid it, until she noticed the bold subject line- ***Mandatory Meeting Tomorrow/ Gala Budget 7:30 am sharp!.***

Fuck, I hate early morning meetings! She thought. The sound of a car pulling in the driveway interrupts her thoughts.

Bekka peeks through the window. Larry is home. She observes him as he pulls the visor down and pats down his salt and pepper hair before exiting the vehicle.

When he enters the house, he is carrying his briefcase and a bouquet of flowers.

"Hi honey, how was your day?" he asks, handing Bekka the flowers.

Bekka murmurs "A busy-busy day, Lar."

"Yeah, I know what you mean," he says, giving her a peck on the cheek.

"My favorite, peonies. Thanks, Lar!"

"If you're hungry there's some leftover pizza on the stove that the kids made at your mother's."

"No, but thanks, babe. I grabbed a bite with Joe after I left the office. I'm stuffed. I have about an hour of work to do before I hit the sack. I'm going straight up to my office."

Larry gives Bekka another peck on her forehead, and brushes her curly hair away from her porcelain skin. Bekka smells him.

"You reek of liquor, Lar."

"That's what happens after a few drinks," he says as he makes his way towards the staircase.

"Ugh, a few? I wish you wouldn't have driven Lar."

"I'm fine, I'm fine, B."

"No, you're just lucky Lar. Try to be quiet while the kids are sleeping."

"I know, I know. I'm just going to peek in on them."

"Oh... and Larry I need the car tomorrow. Early morning meeting at 7:30. So text your mother and borrow her car and take the kids to school."

"Bekka, I have to be in court at 9am," Larry shouts down from the stairway.

"How could you throw this at me at the last minute, when you know I've been prepping this case for weeks!"

Here we go Bekka says to herself. Two people sharing one car always starts an argument.

"Shhh, keep it down! I'm not trying to ruin your morning. Where's the car you keep telling me you're buying, Lar?"

"Yes, B you're going to get your own car, soon. But not tonight. Can you please text my mother and ask her to drive the kids? I'll uber to the courthouse."

"Yeah, yeah" Bekka replies, filling a vase with water. She places the flowers on the dining room table and then heads upstairs.

She looks through her closet for something conservative since Jon Couey, the club President, will be at tomorrow's meeting. She slides the low-cut blouses, and dresses down the rack, out of the way, and settles on a navy-blue knee length skirt and a blouse with a mandarin collar. This is perfect she thinks, holding the ensemble up in front of the mirror. This will keep Jon Couey's eyes from wandering. But I'll still wear my best push up bra and strappy shoes to punish Ted after today's stunt. After all, he will be seated across from Bekka, and he'll shoot her with his gleaming toothy smile. Lastly, she pulls out a satin champagne thong, places everything on the ottoman, sets her alarm and falls fast asleep.

LIV

Tuesday was a busy day for Liv. She attended two real estate classes, did a one-hour exam review and spent the rest of the day running errands, and carting the girls to their after school activities.. It was nearly 10pm when her day ended, and she headed upstairs feeling exhausted.

She kisses the girls good night, texts Jack that dinner is on the stove, and heads to her bedroom. Liv crawls into bed and starts an episode of The Good Wife. Ten minutes later her phone rings.

"Hey, Nat! Perfect timing, I just got the girls in bed. Sorry, I haven't had a minute to call you back. How are you?"

"No worries, I understand. I'm doing well. How are you, Liv? How're the real estate classes going?"

"All good. My classes are going well. Some topics are a bit boring but very informative. I can't believe I only have a few classes left before the exam."

"Boy, that went fast!"

"It sure did! Can't wait to see you and Bekka, Saturday night. I need a break. I need to laugh."

"Yes, me too," giggles Nat.

"What's going on with you, you ok?"

"Yes. I'm ok."

"Are you sure? You sound so blah," admits Liv.

"I'm just in a grey area of my life, at the moment. I'm tired of serial dating. It's been a year since Dean and I broke up and my biological clock is ticking. I don't think anyone really understands that it gets more difficult as women get older. I'm going to be thirty-five in May. Either way, time is of the essence and I'm considering freezing my eggs."

"Hmm, I understand where you're coming from but don't put so much pressure on yourself. Besides, fertility preservation treatments are pretty expensive.

"The truth is Liv; I've been thinking about it for some time. It is expensive and the cost is the only thing holding me up. It runs between five and ten thousand dollars and there's no guarantee. But it gives me hope and a backup plan just in case Mr. Right doesn't come along."

"I know, the expense is a big thing to consider. It involves some financial planning."

Nat agrees, "Yes, it sure does."

"I know the dating scene could be a drag, time-consuming, and a disappointment but I can't imagine that you'll be raising a child on your own. We all have to kiss a lot of toads before we meet prince charming. I really feel like it was easier years ago, before social media. I think social media gives a different impression of a person than who they really are. Everyone is trying to be someone they're not. It truly makes it that much more difficult and time-consuming."

Nat listens intently, and then lets out a soft giggle and replies "I agree. What can I say, everyone wants their cake and they want to eat it too. We all have struggles, and have become more and more selfish. It's daunting."

"Yes, everyone has struggles, Nat. We're all a product of our past. It's all about how we deal with it. Some people accept that they can't change the past and move on. And others let it control the rest of their lives."

"Or, they lie!" Nat chimes in.

"Yes, they lie or they make excuses! Only a man could write a book of excuses!"

Nat giggles.

"Liv, I love that I can talk to you. You always put things in perspective for me."

"Well, your biggest problem is that you have a habit of dating married men. They only guarantee you one thing and that's false hope."

"That's for sure!"

"Are you still seeing Jacob? He's a good catch and adores you, Nat."

"Yes, I am. He really does, and he's a saint. I'm seeing him on Friday, on my day off. He wants to spend the whole day together."

"That's so nice! You need to stop saying yes to married men and say yes more, to Jacob. Stop picking up your phone! Block their numbers! Just stop the insanity!"

"You're right Liv, it is insanity!"

"Turn on Netflix. Join E-Harmony. Change something. Break the pattern! Find a nice Jewish man. I heard they make good husbands. They cater to their wives. Small penis' but good husbands!"

Nat can't stop laughing and mumbles something inaudible.

"What did you say?."

"One of them is calling on the other line," giggles Nat.

"Who?"

"One of the married men!"

"Girl, start now! Engage in a series. Watch Breaking Bad! You'll never hear the phone ringing. That's my advice to you, girlfriend."

"Good advice!" Nat giggles.

"You're the best Liv, thank you! See you Saturday. Love ya!"

"Love ya too. Good night."

BEKKA

(Wednesday)

"Bye Chad, bye Addy. Have a nice day, my sweets. I love you and I'll see you later. Good luck today Lar", she says blowing him a kiss as she grabs her coat and handbag and heads out the door. Bekka arrives at 7:10am, drives through the gates of Mount Tom Country Club, waves to security and accelerates toward the parking lot. She parks in her designated spot, *Reserved for Bekka Newman -Events Director.*

Bekka glances around the parking lot and notices only one other car, Ted's. The nose of his shiny new Range Rover sparkled in the early morning sunlight under the **Ted Gastineau Assistant Vice President** sign. She enters the building, walks to her office passing Ted's without acknowledging him. She hangs her coat, organizes her to-do list and fifteen minutes later realizes it's 7:30 and no one else has shown up for the meeting, not even Jon Couey. Bekka swivels around on her chair and stomps into Ted's office.

"So, what's happening, Ted? No one is here except the two of us."

This was the most Bekka had said to Ted since yesterday's lunch.

"Was the meeting canceled?"

"No, it's not canceled." Ted responds with a smirk on his face. There's a meeting. But it's just the two of us."

"Fuck you, Ted!"

"Relax B, please. I just wanted to be alone with you. I didn't want you to reject me. I haven't heard a word from you since we returned from yesterday's lunch. I understand you feel hurt and confused and I want to apologize to you, face to face."

Ted walks closer to Bekka and puts his hand up around her silky red hair drawing her closer to him as their lips touch. They stood there for a few seconds with their lips locked. Bekka feels Ted's hardness. Her anger and heartbreak start to dissipate.

He locks the door and swings his arm to motion her to the couch. They start kissing, giggling and then Ted kneels. He starts at her right ankle and kisses his way up to her satin panties.

"Oh god" Bekka whispers. "Ted it must be close to eight. People are going to start walking in."

"No worries, we have time. I mentally noted the arrival of each employee so I could plan this meeting" he chuckles. "Now, let's pull this too long of a skirt up. Spread those luscious lollipop legs for me."

Bekka assists him and within moments he is inside of her moving slowly in and out. Then, he gently lifts her legs onto his shoulders moving in deeper and deeper. Perspiration beads down his forehead as he grows more and more excited. He listens to Bekka moan lightly in his ear trying not to be discovered. She leaves Ted's office at 7:55 and heads straight to the ladies' room.

She gives herself a once over in the full-length mirror making sure her skirt is perfect and not wrinkled. She glosses her lips with a light shade of pink complimenting her flushed cheeks, neatens up her hair and walks briskly to her office. She sits down at her desk and tackles her work.

NAT

(Wednesday)

Nat has a busy morning at the jewelry counter and checks her phone on her lunch break. She had five voice messages. Her mother, Elani, Bekka, her landlord, Nino reminding her the rent was past due, and lastly, Gary, a married businessman from LA she's been dating for a few months. He just landed in New York and wants to take her out for dinner. As Nat starts calling her mother, she receives two texts, one from Mrs. Bloomdinger and the other from Jacob. Mrs. B was one of Nat's biggest clients and was coming to see her in an hour. Jacob texts to confirm their plans for Friday. Nat smiles as she eats a salad and reads his text.

An hour later, she returns to work and stays busy the remainder of the afternoon with Mrs. B and a new client selling a few expensive pieces. At five o'clock she locks everything in the safe. She quickly grabs her coat and handbag, and exits the building entering the noisiness of rush hour. As she walks home, she mentally calculates her commission for the day and feels relief that she can pay her rent. As soon as she reaches her apartment, Gary is texting her.

Natalia, what time can I pick you up? I really need to see you. I am staying at the Palace. -Gary.

Nat responds to his text. She takes a quick shower and changes her clothes. Thirty minutes later she climbs into the chauffeured Mercedes parked outside her building and is driven to the restaurant to meet Gary.

"Miss, let me get that for you," the waiter says as he reaches for the napkin and drapes it over Nat's lap.

"Thank you."

Gary stares at Nat. He hasn't stopped smiling since she entered the restaurant and sat down. He orders a fine bottle of wine and some of the specialties on the menu. Nat knows he takes pleasure in ordering since he's a foodie and a silent partner in two of the most popular restaurants in L.A. and Beverly Hills. He is an aristocrat, the heir to the largest European car dealer, 'Archibald Auto' on the west coast. He was blessed with a charmed life and spent years traveling the world until he married ten years ago and had two sons. Gary speaks four languages, one of them being Russian, which he prefers when he's with Nat.

They were driven to the Palace Hotel after dinner. It is Gary's go-to place whenever in New York. They did their usual bump of cocaine on the drive over and walked into the hotel holding hands and laughing. As they kiss wildly in the elevator Nat could feel his hardness pressing against her.

The dinging sound of doors disrupts their heated moment. They enter the room. Gary moves Nat slowly towards the bed, spins her around and gently bends her over. He carefully lifts her skirt and pulls her lace thong down. He gets more excited as he watches it slide down her legs. Then, he enters her slowly and immediately Nat starts to moan. Gary thrusts faster and faster inside of her until he climaxes.

"Wow Gary, this stuff really makes you thirsty!"

"Yes, dry mouth is one of the common effects of cocaine. Here, have another bump, you sexy bitch," he says in Russian.

Nat laughs and takes another hit and then guzzles down a glass of water.

"Just wait and see what happens next," Gary says as he pulls out a pair of handcuffs from under a pillow.

Nat giggles as she jumps off the bed and walks over to the balcony to check out the view. She starts counting stars out loud in Russian as the cocaine takes effect.

BEKKA

Ted & Sympathy (Thursday!)

"Wow, I can't believe he called a false meeting, just to lure you into the office. Men! And then seduces you on the couch. Some balls! I have to admit though; the whole thing sounds pretty hot and it even stirred me up. I may have to go home and jump on Jack. I'll need to get one in so he stays home with the girls Saturday night," Liv laughs.

"More coffee ladies?" the waitress asks. They nod simultaneously.

Bekka gives Liv a quizzical look and puts her hands over her face. "I am so confused, and the guilt is weighing on me. Ted is a great guy and I love and care for him very much but where are we really going with this? I never expected a one-night stand to turn into a relationship for almost two years."

"B, you're definitely overthinking it, or you're getting your period."

"Yes, to both. I guess I'm filling a void in my marriage. Larry is always working and comes home late three to four nights a week. I often wonder where he really is, Liv."

"I would too."

Bekka begins, "Ted, on the other hand, has been working at the club for years. When I started, I never really had any contact with him because his office was on another floor. Once he was promoted to vice president his office was moved to my wing, two doors down from mine. From that point on, we saw each other every day and he would flirt with me every chance he could. If I walked past his office, he would follow me. He'd walk by, wink and say, 'Hey gorgeous!' Non-stop flirting, joking and continuously grazing his hand softly across my back. This went on for weeks."

Liv continues to listen intently as she drinks her coffee.

"Then it happened. The night of the holiday staff party we were all pretty smashed and dancing up a storm at Harlow. Neither of our spouses attended the party. Larry was working that night and Ted said his wife was ill. I swear 'till this day, Ted never told his wife there was a party. A few of us continued to an after-hours place 'til the wee hours of the morning. Ted and I stumbled out of the place together at 2am and headed straight to his car and had sex. I don't even remember half the evening. I swear I had a blackout."

Bekka pauses for a few seconds. She then continues, "When I returned to work the following Monday, I felt embarrassed when I saw him. Since then he hasn't stopped showering me with attention, compliments, lunches, gifts and amazing orgasms. He makes me feel beautiful and happy. He's a gem! I really don't know what I got myself into. Some days I wish it never happened and on days Larry isn't being considerate and respectful I feel happy and deserving I have Ted. He truly treats me like a queen."

Bekka holds back her sadness but pushes through, "Half the time Larry doesn't remember our anniversary, my birthday, or anything I say to him. Ted remembers everything from my last menstrual cycle to how much my haircut was. Lar keeps late nights at the office and comes home with liquor on his breath. I often wonder if we're living separate lives together. I really need some good advice here Liv."

Liv collects her thoughts, "Listen we all have our ups and downs. Marriage is the triumph of imagination over reality."

"That's for sure!"

"Life is too short and we need to be happy. It's so important. I know you must feel guilty about Ted but honestly, if Larry doesn't put time and effort into your marriage then he shouldn't be surprised if it falls apart. Maybe, you're meant to be with Ted. I've always believed there's a reason for everything."

"Yeah Liv, you're probably right."

"No marriage is perfect, B. I have my moments with Jack. He doesn't listen either. He only hears the first three words of every sentence. I think they all tune us out at some point. If two people aren't working on their marriage, then they'll eventually grow apart. Sometimes the person we fall in love with is not the person we stay in love with.

"We all evolve. We all change and sometimes we don't like each other anymore. Just the other night I spent an hour on the phone giving Nat advice. Whether you're married or single there's always something! The most important thing, B, is that you are happy with yourself. You need to focus on you. Try to take one day at a time. It's all about balance. Or you'll drive yourself nuts!" Advises Liv.

"I know. I know. I'm just in a funk. I get like this as the holidays approach. Larry keeps me on a short leash with the holiday spending and it's frustrating. It's the season to be furious instead of jolly. I could only imagine how joyous the holidays would be if I were spending them with Ted. I swear if I had some serious discretionary income a lot of things would change. I would have my own car for starters. You're right Liv, I have to stop overthinking everything.

"Life is too short. We have been blessed with good health, wonderful children, and great friends. Speaking of friends. What's the plan for Saturday night? I need to know the dress code. I have my eye on this sexy black dress that I saw in the window of Dollz & Daisy's. It's on a mannequin with the oversized pink wig and matching metallic platforms," says Bekka.

"Well then, you should get it if it's going to make you happy. But you may want to leave the wig behind. I'm sure the dress will look hot on your size four figure. I, on the other hand, have no time to go out shopping and I hate everything in my closet! I'll do my usual, buy something online, pay for express shipping, or wear something old but good."

"Whatever works girlfriend," Bekka says with a big grin.

"Nat said she's coming to Brooklyn around seven. I was thinking we would start with cocktails at Divine, and then we can eat locally or head to the city. Let's just go with the flow. It will be great to be together and laugh."

"Yes, it will be. I'm excited!"

"Me too," Liv responds, as she glances at her watch. "Hey B, I'm going to head out now. I want to catch the 9am spin class."

"No problem. I need to get into the office anyway. I also need to start hitting the gym. I feel so out of shape."

Liv replies, "you're welcome to join me anytime. The classes are very addicting!"

"I'm sure they are. I will join you after the gala in two weeks. It's going to be another crazy day at the office. The guest list has tripled in size since last year."

"That's a good thing, B! I have class this afternoon. Six more until I take my state test. If all goes well, I'll be finished before Thanksgiving."

"Yay, that's exciting news Liv! It really is!"

"Yes, I'm getting excited."

"Hey Liv, thanks for being a good friend, as always. Venting to a girl-friend always makes me feel better."

"Anytime B. You're welcome."

"Love you and see you Saturday night!" Bekka says as she gives Liv a kiss and a big squeeze.

"Love you too, B."

Bekka leaves smiling like a big weight was lifted off her shoulders.

NAT

Dirty Stay Out (Thursday)

"Drop me on the southeast corner please!" Nat shouts out to the cab driver.

It's nearly 9am and she's running on empty. She's in dire need of a shower, change of clothes, and a strong cup of coffee before heading to work.

Nat decides on a simple dress and a pair of boots. She twists her hair into a chignon and applies more eye makeup than usual to cover up her sleepless night. Thirty minutes later she hails a taxi and heads straight to the diamond district. Thursday's are usually one of her busiest and highest commission days and Nat knew calling out would screw up her finances for a month. So she sucked it up and stopped thinking about how tired she felt.

A text from Gary came in as she exited the taxi and headed towards the revolving doors.

Amazing evening! I hope you will come to visit me in LA next month. I am serious! My wife and kids are in Napa that weekend. We can stay at the Beverly Hills Hotel. Xo. -Gary.

LIV

After the gym, Liv took a shower. As she pulls on her jeans, she hears her phone. DING! There are two missed calls from her mother.

"Hi, Mom, what's going on?"

"What are you doing?" her mother asks.

"I'm getting dressed. I have class in an hour. What's wrong?" Liv asks, hearing the tension in her mother's voice.

"Well, I went to the doctor and he wants me to check into the hospital."

"What? Why?"

"Liv, I haven't been feeling well the past couple of weeks and I've been having a lot of pressure in my chest. It's been waking me up at night and it's not normal. They did three EKG's, and they all came out abnormal so they want me to be admitted into the hospital so they can run more tests as soon as possible. They're afraid something could happen. They may keep me overnight."

Liv couldn't believe what she was hearing. "Oh, no! Mom, why didn't you say anything?!"

"I didn't want you to worry, Liv. I thought it would pass."

"I'm going to head out to you in fifteen minutes. Wait there. I'll take you to the hospital."

"No Liv! I don't want to go. Maybe tomorrow."

"What do you mean maybe tomorrow? We need to go today, Mom!"

"I'm afraid, Liv, if I go, I'm not going to leave."

"Mom, of course, you're going to leave. Please, don't make things more difficult."

"I'm not getting another surgery. No matter what they say Liv. I won't survive. I'm not the same since those two back surgeries."

"Mom, let's see what they have to say first before you make any decisions. It could be nothing. Let me call you back from the road. I need to call Jack and let him know what's going on and arrange someone to pick the girls up from school. Love you."

"I feel bad you have to miss your class. Love you too."

"Mom, relax, please. I'll call you back shortly, bye."

Liv calls Jack.

"Liv, don't worry about a thing. My father will pick the girls up from school and take them to gymnastics."

"There's chicken marinating in the fridge Jack," Liv says nervously as she grabs her handbag and runs out the door.

"Liv!" Jack says with a firm tone. "Like I said, don't worry about anything. Just take care of your mom and keep me updated. I won't say anything to the girls until we know something. Stay with her for as long as you need to. I'm sure she's nervous and wants you with her. You should call your siblings Liv. Let them be involved."

"I can't even think about them now. I will call them from the hospital. Don't worry. I won't deal with it on my own. Thanks, Jack! Speak to you later."

Liv and her mom arrive at the emergency room. A nurse escorts them to a hospital cot where Josie lays down. The nurse draws the curtain and a few minutes later a physician walks in. He introduces himself as Dr. Rue and then starts asking Josie what brought her in today.

While he examines Josie, Liv texts her siblings.

Tess responds immediately- *Oh my god! Is she okay? We will come to the hospital.*

Liv replies- *Yes, yes! Everything is under control. She's in good hands. They're just running routine tests. Once I speak with the doctor, I will update you. No need to rush here.*

Okay. Cody and I are together FYI, xo Tess.

The next couple of hours dragged on. Liv fell asleep in one of the hospital chairs until loud voices and clicking of heels awakened her. A moment later the curtain was drawn.

"Hi Mom," Cody says with a mouthful of bubblegum.

"Hey Mom, how are you feeling?" asks Tess.

"I'm fine, I'm fine. I can't wait to get out of here."

"Are they letting you leave today?" asks Cody.

"They better! I've had enough tests and blood drawn for the next year. I feel like a pin cushion," groans Josie.

They all laugh.

Nurse Caroline walks in to check on Josie. "We should have your cardiogram results soon and if all looks good you will be discharged in an hour."

"Oh, thank goodness! I really want to sleep in my own bed."

"I'm sure you're fine, Mom. Let's be patient and wait for the doctor to give us your results," says Liv in a confident tone as she hears her phone ring.

"Hi girls!"

"Hey, Mom! We have you on speaker. Dad said you're with Mema."

"Yes, I am. She wasn't feeling well. I took her to the doctor. Everything is fine and I should be heading home soon."

"Ok tell her we love her."

"I sure will, my loves'. You can call her later."

"We will. Love you too Mom! Bye."

"Love you more. Bye!" Liv hangs up.

Thirty minutes later, the doctor walks in. "Josie, good news! All your tests came out normal. It may have been gas or anxiety" says Dr. Rue.

"Oh my. Can I go home now?"

"Yes, I am going to discharge you, but I suggest you make an appointment and follow up with your primary in three weeks. Promise me you'll do that."

"I promise, I will. Thank you, thank you," says an excited Josie.

"What a relief! Mom, I'm so happy you're fine" says Cody.

"Yes, we all are," says Tess smiling.

"Girls, I'm so sorry I made you come all the way here for nothing. Especially you Liv, I feel bad. You look exhausted. Why don't you stay over?"

"Mom, please it's no big deal, really. I'm grateful you're okay. I will take you home and then head back. Besides, there won't be much traffic and I want to sleep in my own bed too," chuckles Liv.

It's close to midnight when Liv leaves her mom and heads home. Her phone rings.

"Hey, Jack!"

"Hey Liv, what's going on? I got your texts. How's your Mom?"

"She's ok. All her tests were negative, thank god! They discharged her from the hospital. I'm relieved. I'm on my way home. I can't wait to shower. What's going on with you?"

"I'm on my way home too."

"What? Jack, I thought you were home with the girls by now!"

"I had a late appointment."

"Really? How late, Jack? It's almost midnight. Who's with the girls and what did they have for dinner?"

"Liv, relax! My father is still with the girls. He fed them and he put them to bed. I had a last-minute client. A call came in from ABC. I had to do one of the anchor ladies' hair."

"No one else could have done it?"

"Liv, please!"

"Whatever, Jack! I'm tired."

"Why is everything a big deal?"

"You know Jack, I've had a stressful day! A partner should pick up the slack. The more successful you are, the less time you spend at home with your family!" Liv's eyes start to well up and the tears roll down her cheeks.

"I know, I know Liv. Do I really need to feel guilty? We both had a long day. We'll talk at home. Drive carefully!"

Liv hangs up and opens the window. She feels the cool air dry up her tears as she takes a deep breath. Then, she turns up the radio and sings the rest of the drive home.

NAT

How Sweet It Is (TGIF)

Lying on the bed with her face flushed, Nat is in a euphoric state from her second orgasm. Jacob is staring down at her smiling ear to ear. Nat smiles back.

"OMG that was incredible," she says as she looks into his eyes. She kicks off her Louboutin's and wraps the bed sheet around him.

"I'm hungry babe. Let's order room service and then take a bubble bath."

"Sounds good to me!" she replies, planting a kiss on his lips.

A couple of hours later, they hit the streets to do some shopping. Nat grabs Jacob's hand and squeezes it. Everything is feeling more than perfect, she thinks. When Jacob suggested they spend her day off together she jumped at the opportunity. It definitely beats the heck out of spending the day paying bills and running errands. Besides, she always had an amazing time with him. Aside from his hearing being impaired, Jacob was nice looking, generous, loving, and treated her like a lady. He's Armenian, and the son of one of the most successful jewelers in New York City.

Nat reflects back to when she first noticed him standing in front of the window at the jewelry exchange one morning, about six months ago when she was arranging jewels. Unbeknownst to her, Jacob couldn't take his eyes off her from that moment on. He was mesmerized by her long blond hair with streaks of gold, big blue almond shaped eyes. He looked for her every day from his store window observing when she arrived and left work. Jacob was too shy to approach her until one day, his father asked him to run across to the jewelry tower and drop off a watch to Mr. R.

Jacob was nervous but also excited that this could be the perfect opportunity to meet Nat. He walked across the street and spotted her immediately as he walked through the revolving door. He noticed she was finishing up with a customer. They made brief eye contact, and both smiled. Trying not to be obvious, Jacob started talking to Mr. Rosenthorp, but the old Jew ignored him, cocking his head downward to examine a diamond with his magnification device. Jacob turned on the heel of his Magli shoes and headed towards Natalia's counter. She noticed him walking towards her and she smiled. Jacob managed to get the words out slowly, "Hello, how's your day going, beautiful?"

"It's going very well, thank you. How's your day?"

"Better now" he answered.

They had small talk about the jewelry business. Jacob informed her that he's been working for his father since he was sixteen and knew everyone on the block except for her.

"Well, you can't say that any longer," Nat giggled.

During their brief chat, Jacob pointed out that he was born with a hearing impairment and has been wearing an invisible hearing aid since he was four years old.

Natalia instantly took a liking to him because he was very sweet, forthcoming and made her laugh. A week later they went on their first date to restaurant Daniel. He was a perfect gentleman compared to some of the ego kings she's dated. Most were successful, married, and chronic cheaters.

Others were single, living life in the fast lane, and had commitment phobia. Either way, Nat was bored with the expensive restaurants, fancy hotels, and lonely cab rides home at the wee hours of the morning. She felt a connection with Jacob.

Nat's thoughts are interrupted when Jacob asks if she would like to go to an Italian restaurant for dinner. "Sounds good!"

After dinner, they returned to the hotel feeling giddy from imbibing a bottle of champagne. Jacob picks Nat up, carries her to the bed where he undresses her slowly. He fondles her nipples and works his way down from her breasts, to her vagina using his tongue. For the next thirty minutes, it was pure ecstasy for the two of them.

"Jesus! That was amazing. Oh my, I'm so sore I don't think I'll be able to walk tomorrow," Nat says laughing.

"Maybe, we shouldn't go to work tomorrow. It's Saturday and we can take the whole weekend off!" Jacob says smiling before they fall asleep.

BEKKA

Bekka, frustrated with Larry, exits her house and jumps in an Uber. He had waited until the last minute to tell her he needed the car. She glares out the window yawning, watching cars race through yellow lights and people hustle down the street. Thank goodness it's Friday. My night out with Nat and Liv is something to look forward to. It will certainly relieve some of the stress I endured this week. Bekka exits the Uber and enters her office spending the first half of the day answering emails and calls. During the early afternoon, she has a quick chat with Ted and then breaks for lunch. Upon returning to her office Bekka receives a disturbing text from her friend Sara.

I don't know what to make of this but I thought I'd send it to you since you're much closer to Liv than I am.

And there it was, a photo of Jack lip-locked with his business partner Pepe, on the corner of West Broadway.

"Holy Fuck!" Bekka reacts. She then responds to Sara- *Jesus, I don't even know how I would tell Liv about this. It's truly fucking disturbing! I guess it beats a young hot chick. Fuck, fuck, fuck! I am going out with Liv tomorrow night and I'm definitely not bringing it up until I think this through. I wouldn't be a good friend if I didn't show her. Ugh! Maybe she'll find out some other way.*

Sara replies- *Sorry, I thought it would be best to let you know. Women need to look out for each other, especially the ones we care a lot about. Hopefully, I didn't ruin your day. I'll call you on Monday. I'm at the airport boarding a plane to DC. Ciao.*

Sounds good. Safe travels. Xo.

Bekka spent the remainder of the day doing paperwork and feeling sick to her stomach as she intermittently viewed the photo of Jack and Pepe.

FRIYAY!

Liv yawns as she stretches her legs out from beneath her desk. It's been a long week and agency law is hard to absorb on six hours sleep.

After class, she regains some of her energy, runs errands, heads home to catch up on some chores and prepare dinner. Liv hadn't heard from Jack all day. Must be another busy day at the salon she thought, while she texted reminding him about the girls champion swim meet that evening.

He responds, about an hour later- *Okay see you there.*

Liv arrives at the swim meet and wishes the girls good luck kissing each of them on their forehead. She finds a seat in the first row of the bleachers so nothing would interfere with taking photos, at the most subscribed meet of the season. The excitement loomed in the air, the seats filled up quickly, and people lined the walls to observe. The coach blew the whistle and the meet started. The crowd didn't stop roaring. Liv kept an eye out for Jack, but he was nowhere in sight. Eventually, she calls him. "Hey, Jack!"

"Hey hun, what's going on? Are they winning? It's hard to hear you."

"Yes, they're winning! They're swimming against last year's winning team, the Stingrays. The place is packed like a subway during rush hour. Where are you?"

"I'm still at the salon."

"Oh, Jack!"

"I know, Liv. It was a very busy day. A lot of last-minute walk-ins. I just locked up. Believe me, I'm more disappointed than you are."

What else is new, Liv thought. "Uh huh," she responds, deciding that picking a fight would most likely ruin her girls' night out.

"I'm exhausted and heading home now. Is there anything to eat?"

"There's chicken and rice on the stove. Don't forget I'm going out with Bekka and Nat tomorrow night."

"Yes Liv, I know. I may not be home until after eight. We're fully booked and shorthanded. Patty went out on maternity leave today."

"Jack! I've had these plans since the beginning of the week! I don't want to leave the girls alone!"

"Relax, my father will stay with them. Don't worry, I've already spoken with him. I'll see you at home. Bye!"

"Okay. Bye Jack."

Liv hangs up feeling a bit frustrated until the sound of a whistle interrupts her.

"Tonight's winning team is the Blue Dolphins!" The roaring of the crowd is deafening. Liv quickly tunes back in, clapping her hands as she observes Bea, Nikki, Juliet, and the team receive their trophy.

NATALIA

Diamonds in The Rough

A gunshot goes off. Shortly after, the sounds of sirens were getting closer and closer. A dozen police officers were scurrying outside the revolving door.

The security guard yells out "Everyone is on lockdown until further notice."

"What's going on?" Nat asks her boss Ron in a shaky voice.

"There was a heist across the street at forty-four. It may have been an inside job. Possibly an employee and his accomplice. The accomplice is still on the loose. No one knows if he's still inside or if he fled. Right now, we need to keep everyone safe."

"Oh my! Was anyone hurt? I heard a gunshot. Did they get away with anything?"

"Well, it wasn't a pretty scene" Ron replies.

"I just got off the phone with Dave Shlosberger who witnessed the robbery. Apparently, the thief entered through the back hallway where the restrooms are. He was masked and had a gun. One employee tried to jump him from behind, but the thief was quick on his feet and brutally attacked the employee, shooting him in the chest. He died at the hospital."

"Oh my god!" Nat said as she chewed nervously on her fingernail with tears in her eyes.

"To say the least, the thief was on a mission. He grabbed handfuls of watches and dumped them into a backpack and ran. The police estimated $300k in Rolex, Mullers, and Bucherer's watches were stolen. Trust me, it's not a coincidence he arrived ten minutes before closing when all of our safes were open. I'd say it's an inside job."

"I'm scared Ron! I want to go home!"

"You will doll, I promise. We just have to wait until it's safe to leave. They're still trying to apprehend the thief. They said they're looking for a slim, black male in his 30's, with gray sweatpants, red Nike sneakers, and a blue North Face jacket."

Nat stood nervously gnawing at her nails.

"You know dear, this is why we hire extra security during the holidays when inventory is abundant."

"I know people are desperate. But why do they have to endanger the lives of others?" Asks Nat.

"Because they're on a mission and not thinking about anything or anyone but themselves."

"I hope we're not going to be here all night. I have plans."

"Of course, you have plans, it's Saturday!" Ron replies laughing.

"Don't worry Nat, it shouldn't be too much longer. In the meantime, let's put everything in the safe and lock it up."

"Okay, okay."

LIV

Big Love (Saturday)

"Hey girls, come down for breakfast."

A few minutes later, Liv hears thumping down the stairs. Juliet appears in the kitchen.

"Hi, Mom. Good morning."

"Good morning sweetie. How did you sleep?"

"Like a baby."

"Good," Liv giggles. "Are your sisters up?"

"Nikki's in her room on her phone and Bea is in the bathroom."

"Call them to come down so we can make some pancakes."

"Ok, Mom."

"Love you sweetie."

"Love you too, Mom."

Five minutes later Nikki and Bea enter the kitchen bickering.

"Mom, tell Nikki to stop teasing me!" Bea says waving her hands in the air.

"Girls, what's going on?"

"Bea is being stupid! I have my period and I forgot to flush the bowl. She screamed at me and called me lazy. I have bad cramps! I can't wait 'til she gets her period and sees how it is!"

"Girls, be nice. Let's put some music on and make breakfast!"

Shortly after, Jack enters the kitchen, tosses a pancake in his mouth, kisses everyone goodbye, and leaves for work. Liv spends the day with the girls baking cupcakes, watching a movie, and playing monopoly.

"Hey, Mom, who are you going out with tonight?" Bea asks.

"Bekka & Nat. I'm so looking forward to it. It's been a crazy week."

"I know Mom. I hope you have a good time," says Bea.

"Thank you, sweetie. I feel better now that Mema is feeling better," Liv says with watery eyes.

"Us too," says Nikki as she gives her mother a hug.

"Who's watching us?" Juliet asks.

"Big Daddy!" Liv replies.

The girls laugh.

Juliet notices her mom's watery eyes. "We want you to have a good time tonight and laugh a lot, Mama."

"I know you do, thank you. I love you all so much!"

"I actually need to jump in the shower soon. It's almost five o'clock."

"Can I order the sushi now Mom?" asks Nikki.

"You sure can."

DING! Liv looks at her phone. It's a text from Jack.

What time are you leaving tonight?

Liv- *We're meeting at seven at Bar Divine.*

Who are you going out with?

Liv frowns as she takes in his question.

53

Bekka and Nat. The usual suspects! What time do you think you'll be home, Jack?

I hope by eight, but don't worry my father will be there at 6:30.

Liv feels frustrated and suspicious by Jack's vague answers.

Okay Jack.

Liv heads upstairs to take a shower and get ready. She calls Bea as she starts getting dressed.

"Hey, Mom!"

"Bea, can you come upstairs? I need your opinion on my outfit."

"Okay Mom give me a minute. We're just cleaning up the kitchen."

"Sure, thanks!"

"Mom, I like the jumpsuit the best! You look good! Can I pick out your jewelry?" Bea asks excitedly.

"Of course!"

Bea rummages her mother's jewelry box, and pulls out a pair of chandelier earrings and a sparkly bangle. "Here Mama, you should wear these."

"I will, thanks, Bea."

"I need to head out in a few minutes. Can you grab the silver bag in my closet?"

"Okay. What do you want me to put in it, Mama? I'll help you so you're not late."

"Appreciate it. Money, license, credit card, and my keys. Thanks, sweets."

Liv's phone rings.

"Mom, it's Mema. Should I answer?"

"Yes, please."

Bea has a brief conversation with her grandmother then hands the phone to Liv.

"Hi, Mom. Everything okay?"

"I'm okay. I did feel a little pressure in my chest earlier but like the doctor said it's probably just gas."

"Hmm, okay," Liv replies, still not feeling completely confident about her mother's condition.

"What are you doing, honey?"

"I'm getting dressed. I am meeting Nat and Bekka for dinner. But I can drive out to be with you if you're nervous."

"No Olivia, I'm fine. I didn't call to make you nervous. Go and enjoy yourself. You need a break. I'm fine. Really, I'm fine."

"I hope you're not just saying that, Mom."

"No, I really am, Liv. I feel better. Call me tomorrow. Love you."

"Okay, Mom. Call me if you feel anything. I can be there in an hour. I Love you too. Bye, Mom."

"Mom, you better leave soon. It's almost seven o'clock," says Bea with a tender tone. "I know Bea. I just need a moment." She pauses, then takes a deep breath. "Come here and give me a hug."

"I know Mom. I feel bad that Mema's alone. At least she has Kiko, her crazy cat."

"True," Liv laughs as she hugs Bea and kisses her forehead.

"I love you, Bea. Thanks for helping Mama. I'm ready to go now."

"You're welcome, Mama. Nonno is here so we're going to watch a movie with him."

"Sounds good."

Liv heads downstairs and grabs her jacket. She says a quick hello to her father in law and kisses her girls, goodbye.

"Mommy's leaving. See you all later."

"Bye, Mom."

"See you later Liv. Have fun!" her father in law says. "And you don't need to call. I'll take care of everything. Even this stupid dog. What does he have in his mouth?"

Nikki yells out, "Tito!" as she chases him around the house.

Liv walks out into the chilly air and takes a deep breath.

DING!

Nat texts- *Girls I just got here. Take your time.*

Liv glances at her watch as she waits at the corner for the light to change. It's 7:15.

Liv- *Sorry girls I got caught up. On my way. See you in a few.*

GIRLS JUST WANNA HAVE FUN!

"Hi girls! I'm here!" Liv yells out as she waves her hands in the air.

"So sorry I'm late."

"Hi, Liv! No worries. We're so happy to see you," says Nat.

"Yes! Finally, we're all together!" Bekka cries out.

"I had quite a day. Girlfriends, I thought I'd never make it here tonight."

"I can only imagine. You must have been terrified," says Liv as she gives Nat a hug.

"I was. Believe me, I was."

"I know. I know. Thank god you're okay girlfriend," Liv states with teary eyes.

"Yes, thank God. It freaked me out when I saw it on the news" says Bekka.

"I could not sit still. I paced back and forth in front of the TV until they announced they apprehended the thief."

"Trust me, ladies, I was shaking like a leaf. I would have fainted if it happened in my shop. It certainly was a relief when the police announced it was safe to exit. My legs were still shaky as I walked home. I was numb as I entered my apartment. Then. I jumped in the shower, washed and blew out my hair just to keep my mind off it." Nat replies.

"So that's why your hair looks so good!" Liv says with a soft giggle.

"Poor baby, you must be traumatized. Maybe it wouldn't have been a bad idea to stay home. After all, your mental health is important." Bekka adds as she hugs Nat.

"That's for sure."

"Poor Jacob was worried about me the whole time. Meanwhile, it happened next door to his shop."

"Awe, he's too sweet," said Liv.

"Yes, he is," agrees Bekka.

"Maybe it could have been avoided if everyone wasn't on their phones and distracted. I want to forget it happened. Otherwise, I'll never go back."

"Hmm, that's an interesting thought. Yes, everyone is on their phones" adds Bekka.

"We all have OCD. Literally! The innovation of telephones should have ended with the push button" giggles Liv.

"I remember how excited my mother was when the extra-long spirally cord was invented. They were seventy-nine cents each and sold out in two hours at our local hardware store."

"I remember that! It was in 1981! You weren't even born yet, Nat!" laughs Bekka.

"You're right! "

"Ha-ha, that's funny," remarks Liv.

"Now, we depend on our phones for everything, from bank transfers to tracking cardio activity. I hate it sometimes." says Nat.

"Me too," agrees Bekka.

"Yep! We do depend on them way too much and when they don't function properly our day is topsy turvy" Liv points out.

"True, very true. We're like robots walking around with these devices," adds Nat.

"Exactly, like robots. It's scary! Both men and women are looking more and more alike especially with all this cosmetic surgery. Have we lost our minds? What has this world come to? Everyone looks like a duck," states Liv.

"Ha, ha, ha. That's hysterical Liv, and an unfortunate truth." Bekka comments as she orders another round of drinks.

"No doubt, we're all getting older and a little fine-tuning doesn't hurt. A little Botox, a healthy diet, consistent exercise routine, a good skincare and sleep regimen, eight glasses of water a day, and a glass of red wine once in a while with girlfriends is what works for me!"

"That sounds like a good routine, Liv!" Bekka approves.

"Yeah, that pretty much covers it all!" says Nat.

"The more I look around the more inclined I am to stick with that mantra. Everyone is over injected or so overdone! All I see are frozen faces, no smile lines, no forehead creases and a mouth full of chiclets. Let's toast to aging gracefully, girls!" Liv commands.

"Yes, aging gracefully!" giggles Bekka as she raises her glass.

Nat is laughing as she swiftly lifts her glass. "A mouth full of chiclets. Too-too funny" she blurts out as she spills some wine on her blouse.

"Anyway, thank God you managed to get away unscathed. Bekka and I wouldn't know what to do without you. We love you, Nat!" Liv states in a heartfelt tone.

"And, I love you both too!" responds Nat with watery eyes.

"So, how was the rest of your week, Liv?" Bekka asks.

"The rest of my week?" Liv responds perplexed. "Hmm, busy. A busy week. It started with class and my head in my book. As you both know I am at the tail end of my real estate classes and preparing for my license exam."

"Wow, that's exciting Liv!" Bekka replies.

"Each day things piled up. Then, I had to take my mother to the hospital. A curveball that turned the rest of my week upside down. It was emotionally exhausting!"

"I'm sure it was. Thank god, it was a false alarm" interjects Nat.

"Yes, thank god!" repeats Bekka.

"Yes, I am grateful. She is doing fine."

"Just stay positive, Liv. Think about how well you're going to do when you're a real estate agent. It's so exciting!" Nat adds.

"I am very excited, girls! I've always had an interest in real estate but never had the guts to move forward with it. I just needed to push myself. Fingers crossed. Just need to get over one more hurdle and pass the exam."

"Not to worry. You'll pass with flying colors!"

"Thanks, Nat."

"Yeah Liv, I'm sure you will," says Bekka.

"Before I ask how your children are," states Nat. "I just want to mention I saw Jack the other night. He didn't see me. I was walking across Lafayette, and he was strolling out of Malo's with a male with a goatee."

"Hmm, goatee," says Liv. "That's definitely Pepe, his business partner. Which night was that, if you don't mind me asking?"

"Thursday. It was around 11 pm," Nat mentions, unsure of how this will go.

"I see. That was the day I was at the hospital."

"I don't want to start any trouble, Liv."

"You're not, doll," Liv said smiling, masking her anger and wondering why Jack would lie about his whereabouts.

"So, how are the girls Liv?" asks Bekka, breaking the awkwardness of the conversation.

"They're well, thanks. All doing excellent in school. Getting more and more independent. I just wish they would fight less. But we all went through that phase with our siblings. So why should it be any different now?"

"Right!" says Bekka.

"I did my share of fighting with Elani," adds Nat.

"How are Matt & Addy doing?" asks Liv.

"They're loving middle school. Matt made the JV volleyball team and he's really enjoying it. He has practice every day and he's exhausted between practices and homework. Addy loves her teachers and made some new friends. She's still dancing and swimming! We are all very busy. See Nat, the whole mommy thing is a big job. You really get sucked in and time flies." expresses Bekka.

"Yes, time does fly," agrees Liv.

"I can only imagine. Well, you're both the most amazing moms I've ever known next to my own, of course."

"Awe, thanks, Nat."

"Thank you! That means a lot" adds Liv.

"It's true, girlfriends! Behind every great child is a super Mom! They're all well rounded and have great personalities. They're so much fun to be around. I miss them," admits Nat.

"Yes, they definitely have robust personalities. Well, anytime you want to babysit just let us know" chuckles Liv.

"Yeah, anytime. Then Liv and I can go out," teases Bekka.

"Ha, not without me!" Nat snaps.

"So aside from the burglary, how was your week, Nat?" inquires Liv.

"Yeah Nat, tell us something dirty" Bekka yells out.

They all burst out in laughter.

"Well," Nat giggles. "The week started with Gary, the LA guy and ended with Jacob. I had fun! Sex, shopping, drugs, and dinners with enticing mounds of caviar, expensive champagne and white glove service.

I've been out every night and I'm barely recovered. I'm still bow legged and exhausted."

"Details, details! We want details!" Bekka shouts as she raises her glass. "But first, let's make a toast to health, happiness and our girls' night out."

"I'll toast to that. We really need to do this more often" Liv says.

"Ditto," said Nat.

The three of them giggle, clang their glasses together, and take a big gulp. Liv orders more drinks. "This is the last round ladies before we exit and grab a bite. Otherwise, we'll be stumbling out of this place like three drunken bimbos."

"Agree," says Nat.

"My oh my, so you had quite the sex-fest this week, Nat! And you with Ted, Bekka! Poor me. I didn't even have one orgasm. Not even with myself!" Liv says, a little disappointed.

"To be honest, sex was the last thing on my mind this week until my phone dinged at 7am this morning" Liv giggles. "I set a reminder to give Jack a blowjob just so he wouldn't blow up our girls night out. It's rare but he declined claiming he was exhausted from working eleven hours the day before."

"Rare is right! Lar would never. He said it helps him sleep better," states Bekka.

Nat couldn't stop laughing.

"But good planning on your part. Jack does have a habit of blowing up our plans at the last minute, and Nat and I have to suffer. I hate it when Larry does it to me."

"I know. I am learning to be two steps ahead."

"Good girl!" praises Bekka.

"See the shit we have to think about, Nat?" Liv blurts out.

"You should stay single as long as possible. Enjoy your freedom. Commitment comes with consequences. Continue dating for now and have fun 'til Mr. Right comes along. The grass is always greener on the other side. I would love to be single for a weekend just to taste freedom again. To be able to do anything in a split second. Spontaneously book a flight to Miami, stay out all night, play hooky from work, even have a one-night stand. Oh my, I can't believe I actually said that. Ladies, how great would it be if we could spend a weekend in Miami and stay at the Delano? A room overlooking the pool stocked with Dom Perignon and a couple of doobies."

"That sounds amazing" Nat chimes in. "Marriage and children really weigh you down and change your life and your priorities. It's a life of organized chaos. It's hard to maintain balance. There's always compromise."

"I have to agree with that," says Bekka.

"It all comes down to compromise. Today, women do it all. We raise children, and work. Remember the Enjoli commercial?"

"Yes, I do!" Liv shouts exposing her beautiful teeth.

"Hmm, I don't think I do," Nat says laughing.

Liv and Bekka start singing "We can bring home the bacon, fry it up in a pan and never let you forget you're a man... because I'm a woman... Enjoli!"

Their loud singing grabs the attention of the cast of characters hanging at the bar. They applaud Liv and Bekka.

Liv, Nat, and Bekka laugh so hard they barely notice the two guys next to them staring.

"Hey ladies!" yells the one with dark wavy hair and goatee. "My friend Milo and I were wondering if we can buy you a round of drinks? My name is Nico."

"Ooooh really?" Bekka says slurring her words as she finishes off her mojito. "I think we're good. Right girls? We're going to be heading out in a few minutes to get a bite to eat."

"Yes, we're good. Thanks anyway!" Nat shouts out making a silly face.

"Well, that's too bad," Milo replies.

"Are you sure?" asks Nico.

"Yes, we're sure. We're heading to grab a bite and we want to make it there without falling into a manhole," Liv responds.

They all laugh.

Nat and Nico start talking and carry on until Liv signals her to leave. They say goodbye to the boys and push their way through the thick crowd and exit.

The bar had gotten very crowded. The street was packed with people and vehicles double-parked a block long. Music blared from passing cars, horns honked at the ladies as they crossed the street, and every time the bar door was ajar it sounded like a rock concert.

"Let's catch our breath for a moment, girls and decide where we should have some chow" Liv suggests as she shuffles through her handbag for her phone.

"So, Nat, what were you chatting about with Nico? Did you give him your number?" Bekka asks.

"Of course, Nat says bashfully. I couldn't help myself. After all, he is drop dead gorgeous! I couldn't take my eyes off of him."

"Great eye candy for sure" chuckles Liv. "Handsome he is. Young and beautiful! And in good shape too. His muscle tee shows off those deltoids nicely."

"And the other one, Milo, he's a cutie pie too," says Bekka. "A bit on the short side, but very good looking with a chiseled face and high cheekbones. His Italian accent wooed me. I'll dream of him tonight!"

"Ha, you should! No one is guilty of dreaming. Girls think about what you're in the mood for while I answer a couple of texts from my girls. I didn't hear my phone go off. It was too noisy there."

Liv takes a moment to read her texts. From Nikki and Bea. Ugh! They're fighting.

Nikki- *Bea is not listening to me. I told her to put her laundry away. She hit me.*

Bea- *Nikki thinks she's the boss of me! When are you coming home? I miss you.*

"Here we go. Nikki and Bea are fighting, and Jack is not doing anything about it. He's probably on the couch with the remote and a bag of chips."

"My kids fight with one another all the time. Remember, we did it too. Like you said, why should it be any different." Bekka responds.

"Nikki's been moody since she started menstruating. She speaks to the twins with authority. She fights with Bea non-stop. Juliet is quieter and the more observant one. She's notorious for rolling her eyes and then walking away" laughs Liv.

"I'm feeling a little drunk" Nat blurts out. "I need some water. Can we walk across the street to the deli?"

"I'm feeling buzzed. I haven't eaten a morsel since my one o'clock lunch with Ted," informs Bekka.

"Well, sex only fills you up for so long" laughs Liv. "Yes, let's go to the deli!"

"We did eat! You know I get lightheaded when my stomach is empty. Then, I gave him a blow job."

"In broad daylight?" questions Nat.

"Yeah! We know exactly where to park so no one notices," giggles Bekka as she trips on the cobblestone, landing on both hands, with one foot popping out of her stiletto.

"Oh my, oh my B, are you okay?" asks Liv giggling as she and Nat help her back up.

"Yeah, I'm fine. Like I said I feel buzzed. Need some water."

Bekka holds Nat's hand to steady herself and twist her foot back into her shoe.

"We really need to eat," Liv says.

"Yes, we do," Nat agrees.

"Drinking on an empty stomach is never a good idea. Let's grab a couple of waters and some gum. Should we head over to Galle's for a bit? What do you think girls?" Liv inquires.

"Fine," says Nat, still trying to catch her breath from laughing.

"Works for me," agrees Bekka.

Liv grabs three bottles of water, some gum and mints and places them on the counter.

"Will that be all?" the cashier asks.

"Ladies, anything else?" Liv asks.

"I think we're good," Bekka says.

"Geez, I feel like a mess. It was so hot and crowded in that place. It made my hair all frizzy" Nat says as looks into her compact.

"I got this, ladies," Liv says, extracting her wallet from her handbag.

"Thanks, Liv!" Bekka replies as the flashing neon Lottery ticket distracts her. Hmm, $228 million dollars.

"Girls look, the jackpot is up to $228 million dollars!"

"Is it high enough for us to play?" laughs Liv.

"A matter of fact I think it is. Let's play, girls. You know you have to be in it to win it" Nat adds.

"Yes, let's do it! We have nothing to lose." Bekka says, slurring her words.

"We certainly won't be any worse off," Nat states as she closes her compact and places it in her bag.

Liv grabs a pencil, picks numbers and hands the sheet to Bekka.

"Here, pick some numbers!"

"Hmmm, you picked the numbers that I would have picked," says Bekka.

"Girlfriend, just pick some numbers for god sake and pass it to me! My stomach is growling," giggles Nat.

"Ok, ok, calm down! I guess there's no point in overthinking it" Bekka says as she marks her numbers.

"I'm just feeling light-headed. I didn't mean to snap at you."

Liv pays the clerk, grabs the bag as they exit.

"Here, hold it in your purse" orders Liv as she hands the ticket to Nat.

"Got it," replies Nat.

They walk briskly four blocks to Galle's restaurant.

"Ugh! This place is packed to the gills and my shoes are killing me! I know I must have at least two blisters by now. I knew I should have bought the pink platforms," Bekka said in a drunken raspy voice.

"I disagree. Those shoes are perfect with the outfit. You look so hot!" Nat points out as she pulls a bottle of water from the plastic bag.

"Oh please! You're clearly a MILF! Ted would cum in his pants if he saw you," Liv adds.

"You're probably right about that," agrees Bekka.

"And Nat, you look like your usual movie star self! Those earrings are just gorgeous! I need to have them. I swear you purposely wear everything I'll love just to get a sale out of me," giggles Liv.

"And I think I deserve them after the week I had. Are they expensive?"

"$2900, doll! They're pink sapphires and white topaz. You'll get the friends and family thirty percent off, doll. They're my own design. I sold three pairs this week. They're also available with rubies for $5900."

"Wow, rubies! They must be stunning. When I sell my first house, I'll treat myself to the ruby ones."

"Hey, Bekka, pass me a piece of gum please."

"Here Liv, take the whole pack. The smell of it is giving me a headache."

"Oh, I think drinking on an empty stomach did that," chuckles Liv.

"Hey, if either of you cares to know, I bought this jumpsuit for forty-eight dollars on sale months ago!"

"Wow, where?" asks Nat.

"On Fashion Net. Big sale! Seventy percent off! I couldn't resist after sifting through my closet and discovering how much I hate everything in it, laughs Liv."

"Wow, that's a good deal! It's really nice. Love the fringe hem. I may borrow it some time to wear with the ruby earrings."

"Anytime, Nat," Liv says smiling.

"Now ladies, are you ready to thrust your way through the crowd and see if we can get a table?" asks Nat.

If I don't get food in me soon, I'm going to vomit or pass out" groans Bekka.

"Before we tackle the crowd let me see what I could do. Wait here for a few minutes." Liv says, moving her way through the crowd and waving to a few familiar faces.

"Hi Rick, how are you?" Liv yells out waving her hand in the air drawing his attention from the busty blondes standing in front of him.

"Hello there! Wow, it's been a while. I just saw your husband yesterday at the salon. It's nice to see you, Liv. How are the girls?"

"They're good, really good. Getting big too fast. It's great to see you too, Rick."

"Do you need a table or are you having drinks at the bar?"

"A table please before one of us passes out. This place is a zoo. Nat and Bekka are with me. We just left the zoo at Bar Divine. Drank too much on empty stomachs" smiles Liv.

"So, table for three?" Rick confirms.

"Yes, that would be great. Thank you so much!" Liv says in a flirtatious tone giving him a peck on his cheek.

"Anything, for you, beautiful. Just give me about ten minutes and I'll seat you," Rick replies with a wink.

"We'll be waiting out front. Thanks again!"

Liv pushes her way through the crowd until she reaches the sidewalk.

"We'll have a table in ten minutes."

"Oh, thank you, God!" Bekka says, running a lip gloss wand over her lips.

"So, I gather you found Rick the Armenian hunk?" asks Nat.

"Yes, of course. Rick always takes care of me. Jack and I met him here twenty years ago. We were on our first date. The place has had three facelifts since then. Rick is now one of the owners. The food is mediocre, but the place draws a good crowd. It's the only place we had a chance of getting into without a wait."

"Trust me, I'm not complaining. This place will do" says Bekka.

"We can always go to the city later, girls. After all, the night is still young" Liv assures them.

"Whatever!" Bekka says with an attitude.

"What's wrong with you? You went from laughing your ass off to pissed off!" inquires Liv.

"I'm just getting cranky because I'm starved, drunk and tired. I need to use the restroom."

"Me too, I'll join you," Nat says.

"Well then, I'll wait for you gals at the bar if I make it that far."

As Liv made her way through the crowd and up to the bar, Rick came over and squeezed her shoulder.

"Your table is ready, beautiful."

"Fabulous, Rick!"

"Where are your girlfriends?"

"They took a trip to the ladies' room."

Liv follows Rick to the table, takes a seat, and starts people watching. The bar is a demographic carousel, she thinks. Twenty to fifty-year-old locals socializing. As the busboy approaches the table to fill the water glasses, she notices Bekka and Nat looking around.

"Hey!" she yells out. "Over here, girls!"

Bekka and Nat walk towards the table.

"TPOHA! TPOHA! Toilet paper on heel alert," Liv says giggling as she points down to Nat's feet.

Nat looks down at her shoes and busts out laughing. A long piece of toilet paper is stuck to the heel of her stiletto. She holds onto the back of the chair to steady herself and uses the front of her other shoe to remove it.

"Let's order asap!" Bekka yells out over the noisy crowd.

"Who's our waiter? There should be bread on the table already!"

"Peano-peano," Nat says. "Give him a chance. We just sat down."

"Here comes some bread and olives," Liv says placidly.

"Please let's order food immediately," suggests Bekka.

"Let's do it!!" agrees Nat.

"Good looking crowd tonight ladies. Even the men aren't so bad," giggles Bekka.

"I agree. Lots of hot ladies at the bar. They're pretty, well dressed, and very fit. All the men are loving it."

"Yeah, I'd say!" replies Liv.

"And look at all the gorgeous jewelry, expensive handbags and shoes," points out Nat. "I wish I could afford all of it! I had to refrain myself from walking into Saks on payday and blowing it all!

"Saks, oh I love that store! And Bergdorf too!" Bekka chimes in.

"At the moment, I'm focusing on keeping my priorities in order. Trying to put a few dollars in my egg freezing fund each week therefore, shopping is out of the question. But I am fortunate to have some generous men in my life who love buying me gifts. Speaking of men, remind me to fill you in on Philip Somers. He's a doctor I met two weeks ago," Nat said with excitement.

"We live in a senseless world and we're all to blame for enabling it. It's all about having more and more and more. I really hate myself sometimes! It's only going to get worse. I feel for our children. What will the world be like in ten years?" Bekka says.

"It's all about balance. We are very privileged individuals regardless of the struggles we've each had. Most children today have charmed lives. A lot of people struggle over things that we don't have to think about. It's all relative, isn't it? We've given them all the things we didn't have. Hopefully, they appreciate it. Everything is so normal for them. We've protected them from things we disliked in our own upbringings. I wonder if we're doing more harm than good. I question the decisions I make. It's just not easy. Just not easy," Liv expresses.

"It's definitely not," agrees Bekka.

"I can't believe how crowded the bar is. How can anyone enjoy themselves standing three feet away from it and being pushed in every direction?" Nat blurts out as she puts a forkful of grilled octopus in her mouth.

"Yes, it's crazy. Thank god we got a table. It beats eating at the diner.

"Hey, that looks like Rob Cinti at the bar?" Liv points out.

"Aha!" Bekka yelps, squinting in the direction of the bar.

"Yeah, that's him! So gross! He's all over that big-boobed blonde. Behaving like a bachelor. He's about thirty pounds heavier than the last time I saw him," Bekka mumbles as she chews on a piece of bread sopping with olive oil.

"Last Summer, I heard through the grapevine he put himself on Tinder and was busted by his wife's friend. So, busted! As far as I'm concerned, he should be eating humble pie!" States Liv. Remove this sentence.

"He's a jerk! Thinks he gets to do whatever he wants. His wife Sarah is sweet. I really like her. I see her at the gym working out with her trainer. I feel like heaving every piece of bread in the basket at him" Bekka says in an angry undertone.

"Anyway, who cares! You can't fix stupid," Nat chimes in.

"No, you can't! Men are too stupid to even know what that means," laughs Liv. "I've come to the conclusion there is something wrong with all of them."

"Yes, I agree. Therefore, let's change the subject.

So Nat, tell us about Dr. Phil," Bekka inquires.

"Tell us about him and whatever happened to Harry, the one that owns the restaurant in Little Italy?" asks Liv as she raises her martini glass and takes a sip.

"Oh, Harry is still around. He disappears and resurfaces every few weeks."

"Ladies, I would like to offer you another round?" The waiter says, clearing his throat.

"Sorry, we didn't mean to ignore you," says Nat.

"The guy at the bar with the dark pinstripe suit is buying."

"What guy? We can't even make out who's who. It's so mobbed!" Liv yells out.

"The one with the salt and pepper hair on the left?" the waiter responds smiling.

"The one with the orange murse?" Bekka says in a sarcastic giggly tone.

"Oh, who cares! Sure, we'll have another round. Tanks, I mean thanks," Bekka slurs.

They continue watching and laughing as they share some appetizers.

"So, tell us about the doctor Nat."

"Well, I met him one night at a restaurant in Nolita called Rigala. I was waiting for Dayna to get off work and he was at the bar. He's very nice looking. In his fifties, separated with two kids. His wife lives in Paris with them."

"Hmm, what kind of doctor is he?" Bekka asks.

"He's a doctor that specializes in healthy aging."

"Really, exactly what does that mean?" giggles Liv.

Nat props herself up, hands on waist, and responds, "He basically removes the signs of aging from your face. Age spots, lower eyelid hollowness, saggy jawline, wrinkly lips, furrow lines, etc. He uses Botox, Juvéderm, chemical peels, microdermabrasion, lasers and so on. He has an in-house nutritionist who designs healthy eating plans for each client. He seems to have a pretty successful business.

He wants me to visit his office next week and give me a tour and promised sample creams. We went out on two dates, two weeks ago. Then he left for Paris to visit his kids. He's returning tomorrow. He's a total gentleman."

"Well Nat, I suggest you keep Dr. Healthy-Aging around for a while. You don't need a thing being in your thirties, but your two soul sisters here would love to indulge in some Botox and microdermabrasion at a discount," Liv says giggling, pointing her finger in Nat's direction.

"Yes, that's for sure. I want the eleven removed between my brows and some of the dark spots on my cheeks. Yes, please keep him around for a while," Bekka states, smiling.

"Okay. We'll see!" replies Nat.

"Hey girls, I'm full! Should we finish our drinks and head out? Hit the city while the night is still young. What are your thoughts, sisters?" inquires Liv.

"It's only 10:48, I'm in!" responds Bekka.

"I'm game for anything! How will we get there?" asks Nat.

"My big wheel. It's fucking parked out front!" Liv shouts out as they all laugh.

"Let's see if we can grab a cab out front. Otherwise, I'll call an Uber," suggests Liv as she signals the waiter for the check.

They pay the check, hit the restroom to freshen up, then hustle through the crowd and exit the restaurant.

"It feels so good to be outside. Doesn't it, girls? That place was so stuffy. The fresh air will sober us up," Nat states in her sweet Russian voice.

"Along with six glasses of water and good night sleep," Liv adds.

"Ew! Ew! Look over there!" Bekka screams out as she grabs onto Liv's wrist to balance herself.

"There's a yellow taxi across the street dropping someone off. Let's grab it!"

"Well, look at that!" Nat yodels.

"The timing could not have been better. A yellow cab right in front of us. Well, I'd say it's meant to be girls! We're heading to the big apple," Nat says as she pumps her hands in the air above her head.

"Yes, it's a sign. Now, let's go!" Liv says, skipping into the street to flag down the taxi. "Hi there, we're going to the Meatpacking District," Bekka informs as they all pile in.

"You can drop us off at 14th and 9th Ave."

"Ok ladies. You got it" responds the driver as he hits the gas pedal.

"Shit. My coat is caught in the door," moans Bekka.

"Open it quickly and I'll pull your jacket up," suggests Liv.

"Do you really want to go to the Meatpacking District?" Nat squeaks out.

"Well, where do you suggest? It is almost eleven o'clock" Bekka says with a bit of an annoyed tone.

"No, it's fine. It's just such a crowded part of the city."

"Any place worth going to on the weekend is going to be crowded," Liv comments, staring out the window.

"True," says Nat.

"After all, we can't stay out too-too late. I feel a headache coming on," Bekka groans.

"Ugh! Here we go," Liv says giggling.

"Here comes the whining. Are you going to get car sick too?" teases Nat.

"Not if the driver slows down. He's going way too fast. The car feels like it's all over the road," whines Bekka.

"Just watch the TV screen so you're distracted" suggests Nat.

"Good idea." Bekka groans as she turns her attention to the TV screen.

"Look who they're interviewing, ladies. That Jersey housewife Teresa something. She just got sentenced to fifteen months in prison because of her husband," yawns Bekka.

"Wow, she looks gorgeous! At least she put his money to good use. Clearly the work of a good plastic surgeon," Nat states.

"Yes, she does look good. You'd never know she was under duress. She looks young, healthy and happy. But remember girls, money doesn't buy happiness. She's going to spend some time away from her beautiful daughters. They're young and need their mommy," Liv says in a heart-breaking tone.

"Ladies, the bridge or the tunnel?" the driver shouts out.

"The tunnel!" Nat and Liv yell simultaneously.

"I need to crack the window and get some air," Bekka says as she puts her head in her hands.

"Just chill. We're almost there. A few more minutes and we'll be out of the tunnel," Nat confirms.

So much for the housewife distracting us, Liv thinks to herself.

"Shhh, the news is on! I want to hear the weather for tomorrow. I'm hoping to feel good enough to ride."

"Oh, you and that riding. Can't you skip one weekend? You should stay in bed tomorrow. Sleep late," Bekka recommends in a grumpy tone.

"Girls, they're going to announce the Lottery numbers in a few minutes. Where is the ticket? Get it out!" Liv shouts out.

Good question?" says Nat. "I don't recall putting it in my purse."

"I have it, girls! Go in my wallet. I need some fresh air," Bekka informs as she rolls the window down.

"Eew, love the bag, B. Chanel, nice! Is it new?" Nat asks as she lifts the notch to open it.

"Thed give it to ma for Valentine Dah" Bekka spits out.

Nat pauses and makes a face trying to figure out what Bekka is trying to say. She laughs, "What the fuck did you just say?"

"I'll translate," says Liv.

"Ted gave it to her for Valentine's Day!"

"Did he give you those shoes too? There's a Swedish fish stuck to the bottom of your left heel!" Nat blurts out as she tosses her head back and giggles.

"Wha?" says Bekka.

"Wha about feesh?"

Liv glances down at Bekka's left shoe. She sees the flattened red gummy fish and busts out laughing as she looks over at Nat.

They both laughed harder and harder until tears rolled down their cheeks.

"Whada fuk is so funny and how muk longa? I feel so dizzy." Bekka says in a sleepy voice and then belches.

"Geez B, we're definitely not letting you read the numbers off. You can't even speak, let alone see clearly. Yuk! It smells like octopus and garlic. Can you at least say "excuse me"?" Nat politely asks.

"They're going to announce the numbers now. Get that ticket out!" Liv demands as she wipes her wet cheeks.

"Ha much longer till wa there? I feel so dissy."

"A few minutes. We're halfway through the tunnel" Liv replies, trying to distract Bekka from tossing her cookies. She laughs at Bekka's drunken state.

"Hey Nat, I'll read the numbers off and you check the ticket. Besides, I can't find my glasses. I think I left them at the restaurant. I lose a pair a week" Liv blurts out.

"Ok, ready here we go-- six, twelve, twenty-one, twenty-eight, thirty and forty eight! Liv yells out hastily and takes a pic with her phone before the numbers disappear.

Suddenly, BOOM! Sounds from the back of the taxi, and then the car begins to teeter.

"Wha the fock was that?" Bekka yells out in a hoarse voice. She stares at the back of the driver's head waiting for a response.

"Uh don't know, ma'am."

"The taxi feels like it's leaning to one side. Don't you think it would be a good idea to pull over? Just poool over!" Bekka commands.

"Ma'am, we're still in the tunnel. I can't possibly pull over without causing a collision. As soon as we're out I will."

"Grrr," Bekka moans.

Feeling the sway of the car, Liv stares out the window grasping the door handle until she sees the openness of the starry sky and streetlights.

Finally, the taxi exits the tunnel onto the congested west side highway. Liv lets out a big exhale.

In the meantime, Nat stares at the lottery ticket, silencing everything around her. She checks the numbers off the screenshot on Liv's phone.

The taxi starts swaying from one side to the other. The driver puts the flashers on attempting to pull over.

"Damn it! Pull over before we all get killed!" Bekka screams out at the driver as the taxi sways close to a car in the right lane.

Liv screams out nervously as she witnesses the taxi come within inches of the other vehicle.

"Please pull over sir! Please!" Liv yells out.

"It's too dangerous to pull right here, Ma'am. I need to get away from all of the cars otherwise I will cause an accident."

"Oh my god! Oh my god! Oh my god!" Nat screams out.

"Well, well, look who tuned back in," says Bekka. Did you just realize we're in danger? We're all over the road. Oh my god is all you can say?"

"I can't breathe! I can't breathe!"

"Ladies, relax. I'm pulling over now," the driver shouts out.

"I can't breathe," Nat says.

"He's pulling over Nat, relax!" Liv says, glancing at her.

"I can't breathe!" Nat repeats.

"What do you mean you can't breathe?" Liv asks.

"He's fucking pulling over. We'll be out of the car in a second" Bekka snaps as Nat places her hand over her chest.

"Girls, girls, please. Please listen to me. This has nothing to do with the taxi. I'm having trouble breathing."

"Are you serious Nat? You were fine a few minutes ago. Do you feel sick? Are you pregnant? Tell us" Liv insists.

"Noooo, no. I'm not sick. Nothing like that! She says holding her hands on her chest. You're not going to believe it!"

"What? Let it out already before I shake it out of you," Bekka demands impatiently.

"We. We. we..."

"We what? Spit it out! repeats Bekka.

"We fucking hit the jackpot! Girls, we won the lottery! We won! We won! We're rich! Two hundred and twenty-eight million rich!" Nat says as she gasps for air.

"Nice try, girlfriend! That won't win you an Oscar. Stick to your day job," Liv says as she carefully grabs the ticket planted between Nat's hand and chest.

"Yeah, really Nat, nice try! I'm pissed off enough from this joy ride to the city" expresses Bekka.

"Holy shit! Holy shit! Ahhhh!" Liv screams at the top of her lungs as she opens the car door and jumps out onto the sidewalk.

Nat jumps out next, throwing her arms around Liv. They're both screaming at the top of their lungs. A few moments later they start crying and then jump up and down in a circular motion. Bekka stumbles out of the car, pukes and falls onto her hands. The contents of her handbag spill out onto the street. The driver runs to her side to help her up.

"Are you okay, Ma'am?"

"Damn it! My heel snapped off," Bekka moans as the driver helps her up.

Nat and Liv are hysterical, laughing at Bekka as she stands up wobbling with a shoe in one hand and a heel in the other.

"You think it's funny, huh? You two drunken bitches!"

"You're ridiculous! You're the drunk one! Obviously too drunk to comprehend what's going on!" Screams Nat.

Liv takes a few steps towards Bekka, grabs her leg and removes her other shoe.

"Ay, what do you think you're doing, missy? Give my shoe back!" Bekka demands. Liv swipes the broken one out of her hand then skips over to the garbage pail and tosses them in.

"Problem solved!" Liv yells out.

"You biatch! Those shoes were seven hundred dollars! They could of been repaired by Vinny the shooooemaker."

"Are you fucking kidding? You just won the fucking lottery! The fucking lottery! Earth to Bekka! You can buy all the shoes your heart desires!"

"The Lottery?! The two of you have really lost your minds. You really feel like playing with me all night, don't you?"

"We're not playing. Come and see for yourself!" Nat suggests in a trembling tone.

"Liv and I checked the numbers a dozen times over. We fucking won! We hit the jackpot! Believe it or not!"

Barefooted and drunk Bekka wobbles onto the sidewalk next to Nat and Liv. "Give me the ticket," Bekka snaps.

"Only if you promise to handle it with care" Liv warns.

"Yes. For God sake! Hand it over! I have a migraine."

Nat and Liv stood there with their arms folded smiling ear to ear, as they observed Bekka's reaction. She went from a deer in headlights to a deer in front of a pool full of nuts.

Bekka starts screaming, crying and running around in circles with her hands in the air. The driver turns his attention away from fixing the flat tire and stares at her.

"Holy shit! Holy shit, sisters! We did it! Now, I can't breathe! We did it! We got what we deserve! Our dreams are coming true, biatches! Oh, my fucking god!" Was the last thing Bekka said before returning to puking viciously on the sidewalk. In no time, her shiny red toes were covered in it.

Liv and Nat ran to her side to assist her as she keeled over. They took turns pounding on her back until she was finished.

"Oh my, I'm glad that's over!" Bekka mumbles as she lifts her head and forces herself upward.

"A bad combination of alcohol, mediocre food, a rollercoaster taxi ride, and traumatic emotional shock rolled up in one. Anyone have water?"

"Uh, no," giggles Nat.

"But we can surely get some. Here are all of the tissues I have in my bag," Nat says, handing them to Bekka.

"Wipe your mouth and feet and we'll pay the driver and call an Uber."

"Good idea" Liv agrees as she pulls out her wallet.

"Thank you and good luck with the tire sir."

"Miss, Miss are you sure? I will have the tire fixed in a few minutes and can take you anywhere. I am very sorry for the inconvenience" the driver responds in a soft Indian accent.

"We're good, but thanks anyway. Besides, we've had a sudden change of plans. Thank you again and good night" Liv responds in a pleasant tone as she walks away.

"The Uber will be here in three minutes on the southeast corner of Rector Street," Nat points out.

"Okay girlfriends let's go! My headache miraculously disappeared and I'm feeling better. I suggest skipping the meatpacking district and heading to the Plaza Hotel to have our own party. After all, we're not going home tonight so let's indulge in a place we can afford!" says Bekka laughing.

"What about your children? The husbands? They'll be worried" questions Nat.

"We can settle all that with one phone call," says Bekka.

"Larry is never going to believe me anyway. He'll think I'm drunk and making excuses not to come home. And, he won't be able to sleep late like he normally does on Sundays. He'll be driving Chad to a volleyball tournament tomorrow morning at 7:30am."

"Yeah, you're right, girlfriend! Jack won't believe me either. It will take some convincing on my end for sure. If it was the other way around, we wouldn't believe them either." Liv states.

"You're right, Liv!" Bekka laughs.

Nat giggles as she listens to Bekka and Liv's chatter. "I don't have to go home for a week, and no one would be pissed off. Oh, the advantages of singlehood," she blurts.

"They'll think we're with other men," Liv adds with a grin.

"Let them think what they want!" proclaims Bekka.

"Besides, how long could they possibly stay mad at us, Liv? They're married to very rich women! The longer they stay mad the longer it will take for them to get their share," Bekka rationalizes.

"I fucking love it! I have to tell the two of you, I love it!!! We're now in a position of fuck you. Life at the level of fuck you!"

"What do you mean B?" Nat asks.

"Yes, what do you mean?" repeats Liv.

"We only do what we want to do when we want to do it! Life, at a level of fuck you. Someone wants you to do something you don't want to, fuck you! Your boss pisses you off, fuck you! Live life from the beautiful position of fuck you! We're in complete control of our lives and no one, and I mean no one can tell us what to do! That's what it means, girls. Simply that!"

"Well," Liv says. "That sounds good to me."

"Me too. I still can't fucking believe it." Nat repeats.

"Trust me, it won't take long for us to get used to the good life. We're just getting started!" Bekka comments.

"Look, our car is here. And it's perfect! A shiny black Yukon with blacked out windows. Girls, here's to our new lives." Bekka says as she grabs Nat and Liv's hand and raises them high in the air. Before entering the Yukon, together they look up at the stars as a cool breeze grazes their faces.

"Good evening ladies. How are you tonight?" asks the handsome Afro-American driver with pearly white teeth and a goatee.

"Well, girls, how are we? The driver is asking" Nat sings.

"Over the fucking moon!" Bekka screams out as she opens the window to take in the fresh air like a dog.

"We couldn't be better! This is just about the best night of our lives. The best, best ever!" Liv says triumphantly.

"Really, well that's wonderful. So where am I taking you lovely ladies tonight?"

"The Plaza Hotel!"

"Yes, the Plahhhza," Bekka repeats with a slight Massachusetts accent.

"You got it, ladies! My name is Jaxon by the way. Jaxon with an x," He states proudly.

"That's cool," says Liv.

"Ladies, is there a specific artist or song you would like to listen to? I have everything your ears desire" laughs Jaxon.

Liv hums aloud with pursed lips.

After a few moments she requests, "How about 'Here Comes the Weekend', by Pink?"

"You got it!" Jaxon replies gleefully as the song starts up.

"Eh oh, Eh oh! We don't want no problems! Eh oh, eh oh," the girls bellow out. "Eh oh, eh oh I just wanna play big city holiday!"

"We're ticking like a bomb, about to blow" Liv sings on.

"Eh oh, eh oh," Nat and Bekka chime in as they huddle together cheek to cheek beaming with delight.

"Bravo ladies, bravo!" Jaxon yells over the music as he glances into the rearview mirror with smiling eyes.

"So, ladies, I'm assuming from your enthusiasm you're out of town-ers and it's the first time staying at the Plaza?"

"No! We're native New Yorkers, Jaxon. We've visited the hotel before, but we've never had the privilege of spending the night. But tonight, we are! So, I guess you can say it's our first time. Right girls?" squeaks out Bekka.

"Yes." agrees Nat.

"Yes, it certainly is," adds Liv.

"Oh, nice! I'm sure you'll very much enjoy it" says Jaxon as he drives towards the entrance of the hotel.

It's such a magnificent place! A world renown American landmark. I've never spent a night here either, but my wife and I have enjoyed many lunches right there in Grand Army Plaza. We enjoy the music and everything buzzing around us. It's so captivating!" Jaxon expresses.

"That's sweet! It is a beautiful place and even more breathtaking at night." Nat says, peering out the window with her eyes wide open.

"It's just magical during the holidays. You know girls since my birthday is a couple of weeks before Christmas, we should plan on returning. After all, our landscape has changed" Bekka states as she hiccups.

"Yes, it has and it's just the beginning" laughs Liv.

"It's certainly magical during the holidays. And here we are, ladies, at New York's finest. Is there anything else I can do for you?" Jaxson asks.

"I believe we're good. Unless, you're available to drive us around over the weekend?" asks Bekka.

"Sure! I do have private clients outside of Uber. I'm happy to give you ladies my business card."

"Yes, pleeease!"

"Smart," condones Liv.

"Here you go, ladies! I charge two hundred and fifty dollars for five hours and forty dollars for each additional one."

"That's it?" Bekka quips.

"Well, well, listen to the poor little rich girl," Nat remarks giggling.

"If you didn't hit the jackpot, you'd be blowing your top right now."

"True, but we wouldn't be here in the first place! Since money is no longer an object it sounds reasonable" Bekka says.

Jaxson parks the SUV at the foot of the hotel. The porter gracefully opens the car door. "Thanks, Jaxson, we'll be in touch!" Bekka says in a bubbly tone, as she carefully climbs out of the vehicle barefoot.

"Here you go!" Jaxson says.

"Thank you and have a great evening."

"You too, ladies. Enjoy yourselves and don't hesitate to call if you need anything. Good night."

THE HOTEL

"Good evening, ladies," says the porter. "Welcome to the Plaza Hotel."

"Good evening," mumbles Bekka.

"Girls, let's check in and get settled. Then, we'll order some champagne. For the time being, we'll be living off our credit cards. I have a ten-thousand-dollar credit line on my Amex. What about you girls?" asks Liv as they climb the stairs to the hotel entrance.

"At the moment, I have a five-thousand-dollar limit. Amex has offered me the platinum card. I declined because of the costly annual fee. But, I suppose I could change my mind," giggles Nat.

"I have fifteen thousand, but God knows the damage Larry has done this month," says Bekka.

"I know he dined at the 21 Club, Morimoto, and The Palm the last two weeks. Supposedly he was entertaining clients."

"Wait a moment, girls," Bekka says with her hands up.

"Wait for what?" Nat asks.

"Let's walk over there to Bergdorf Goodman."

"Right now? For what? They're closed" laughs Liv.

"I don't have shoes, remember?"

"Yes, of course! But you can't buy shoes now."

"But, I can window shop! If I see something I like, I can have it delivered in the morning."

"True, very true. Let's go!"

"I'm certainly not going anywhere until I have shoes on my feet, especially to Bergdorf. I'll be the laughingstock," announces Bekka.

"The laughingstock? Did you ever see what the BG clientele looks like?" asks Nat. "They look like over injected Barbie dolls doped up on Oxycontin. I guarantee no one will notice you're barefoot."

"You're probably right." Bekka chuckles.

"Well, then, let's browse the windows, girls. It's a perfect evening and we must enjoy it to the fullest," states Liv.

Bekka tiptoes up to the window.

"Look at that gorgeous gown. Oh my, what a work of art. It's a Valentino! It was featured in this month's Bazaar," Liv mentions.

"Yes, it is lovely. I'm sure it costs a pretty penny!" Bekka toots.

"And look at the shoes, girls. Metallic grey leather peeky toes platforms. The perfect shoe that won't give me back pain. They're perfect with any outfit" continues Bekka.

"Yes, they are beautiful!" says Nat.

"I'll order them in the morning. They'll do the trick until my feet get tired and I find something more practical to stroll the city in. Like a pair of Golden Goose sneakers."

"Yes, seven hundred dollar sneakers are definitely more practical." says Liv.

They were bedazzled by the windows as they stared, admiring every detail. The apparel, shoes, and accessories were beautifully displayed to attract an affluent eye.

"Girls. Girls let's hold hands. Deep breath in and big exhale" Nat says, recalling last month's yoga class.

For a few seconds, they close their eyes and share the energy from their serendipitous evening and look up to the sky to admire the bright twinkling stars above.

"I think it's time we check in, girls. Besides Liv, we need to tell Larry and Jack we're not coming home," Bekka insists as they walk towards the hotel.

"Shoot, I almost forgot about that! I think you just killed my buzz, girlfriend!" says Liv as she retrieves her phone out of her handbag.

"On second thought, maybe we should wait until they call us B. It's almost midnight and I'm sure we'll be hearing from them soon. They're never going to believe a word that comes out of our mouths."

"True. How are we going to prove it to them?"

"Hmm, let me give it some thought" Liv responds as the bellhop holds open the door.

"Ladies, make your first left and go down the hall to the front desk."

"Thank you," says Nat.

"Hey, I have an idea."

"What is it, Nat?" Bekka and Liv ask simultaneously.

"Let's send them a pic of the Lottery ticket and the TV screen. I bet in less than five minutes you'll get a call."

"Great idea, Nat!"

"Let's check in first. See if there are any vacancies. After all, it is a Saturday night," Liv states.

They walk briskly through the marbled floor entryway and pause to admire the iconic "Palm Court" dining room.

"Wow, this room is just breathtaking," Nat says.

"It certainly is," agrees Liv.

"Looks like Central Park, but indoors," chuckles Bekka.

"Look at the detail in this room. And, the soaring palm trees. It's magnificent! Beautiful furnishings, chandeliers, and tables set to perfection with custom linens and china. Just exquisite!" Liv points out as she takes in the beauty of the room with her eyes.

"Well...we'll be sitting pretty there tomorrow, ladies. Now, let's go," Nat says, leading the way to the stunning lobby that showcased the largest chandelier she's ever seen.

"Bonsoir Mesdames," says the front desk clerk.

"How may I help you this evening?"

"Well, good evening" slurs Bekka.

"We would like to know if you have any availability this evening?"

"For how many nights, Madame?"

"One. Possibly two."

"Ok, let me take a look. One moment please."

"Well, Madame, we have three rooms left. Our standard room on the fifth floor has a king bed, our Eloise suite on the eighteenth floor has a king and a full bed and lastly, our exquisite giraffe suite on the nineteenth floor is available. It boasts two king beds, two full baths with jacuzzi, a private terrace, two-sided spectacular view of Fifth Avenue & Central Park and your own private butler."

"Jesus, I think I'm going to faint," Liv says softly.

"I can't believe it myself. Pinch me! We must be dreaming," adds Nat.

"I know, I know it is numbing. A numbing reality. Did this really fucking happen to us? We're actually going to spend the night at the Plaza or is this a dream? We fucking hit the lottery," Liv whispers to Nat as she overhears Bekka speaking to the clerk.

"We'll take the giraffe suite!"

"Okay Madame, the giraffe suite it is. I will need a credit card when you're ready."

"Sure, just one moment. Girls, girls whose credit card should we abuse first?"

"How about yours? We'll save ours for the shopping extravaganza tomorrow!" suggests Liv.

Bekka agrees and she hands over her card to the clerk.

"Merci Madame. How many keys would you like?"

"Three, please. Thank you."

"Here you go. You're all set, Madame. The elevators are straight ahead on the right. Take it to the 19th floor. Your room is 19G. Breakfast is served from 6am to 11am in the Palm Court. Your butler's name is Max. Enjoy your evening, ladies!" the clerk says graciously as he hands Nat the keys.

"We sure will. Merci!"

"Let's go girls!" Bekka says as she twirls around towards the elevators. Her phone dings.

Bekka checks her phone.

"What's up B?" Liv asks.

"Text from Larry. Naturally, he doesn't believe a word I said and is accusing me of being drunk."

"That's his problem," Nat responds as the elevator doors fly open.

"So just respond. I am drunk and I won the lottery!" Liv says giggling as she presses nineteen on the elevator panel.

"He wants to know when I'll be home."

"Tell him at midnight" Liv responds.

"He said it's already past midnight."

"Tell him midnight on Monday, Ha-ha."

"That's a good one. I will," Bekka says laughing.

"It's my turn," Liv says as her phone starts to vibrate.

"Girls, let me talk to Jack before we enter the room. I want to walk in together. After all, it's a moment we'll never get back."

"As long as you make it quick, Liv!" Bekka snaps as she sauntered down the hallway enjoying the plushness of the carpet on her bare feet.

"Hello, Jack."

"What's going on Liv? What's with the pic of the lottery ticket? Where are you?" Jack says over the phone.

"Well, Jack, which question do you want me to answer first?"

"Sorry Liv, go ahead."

"You're never going to believe it! What I'm about to say. It's just unbelievable!"

"Liv, spit it out already!"

"We fucking hit the jackpot, Jack!!! Believe it or not! We played numbers tonight. We stopped at a deli to buy water and bought a ticket. A couple of hours later when we were in a taxi heading to the city the news was on and they announced the lottery numbers. We fucking won! We're rich! Two hundred and twenty-eight million rich."

"Come on Liv, are you playing a joke on me?"

"No joke! No joke!"

"Who else knows?"

"Larry! He's pissed and of course, doesn't believe Bekka. He thinks she's drunk."

"Well, Liv, when isn't she?"

"Is this for real?"

"Yes, I swear on our dogs, Jack! I know it's hard to believe and I can hardly digest it myself. That's why I sent you a pic of the lottery ticket and the numbers so you can see for yourself."

"Holy shit! Holy shit! I think I'm dreaming. Way to go, babe! This changes everything. Jesus! Holy Mary! When are you coming home?"

"I'll be home sometime on Monday," Liv says excitedly.

"Monday? Where will you be all weekend? What will I tell the girls? I'm working tomorrow."

"Jack please, ask your father to help out. We just checked into the Plaza Hotel."

"The Plaza Hotel?!"

"Yes, we're going to stay here and celebrate. After all, we can't collect our winnings till Monday. I will call the girls in the morning and explain. We'll be in room 19G if you need to reach me. We're just walking in. Got to go! Call you in the morning! We're rich! We're rich! Fucking millionaires! Millionaires, do you hear me, Jack? Millionaires! You're the husband of a Millionairess!"

"Wow, I can't believe it. It's amazing! Okay Liv, have fun, be safe and don't go crazy."

"Good night Jack, love you!"

"Love you too! Good night!"

"Ready girls? Let's do it!" Liv yelps as she slides the key card in and slowly opens the door.

"Wow!" Nat screams out.

"OMG, this is pure fabulousness!" Liv squeals, skipping through the entry hall.

"OMG! Nothing compares to this! Not any hotel I've stayed at with Ted," Bekka screams.

"Oh my, check out the moldings and the wallpaper. Everything is so regal. The walls have silk on them," Nat says as she runs her hand alongside them.

"Girls, girls come check out the bedrooms! Feel the bed linens. They must be a thousand thread count" giggles Liv.

"A thousand thread count? Does that even exist? You're a hoot Liv!" Bekka states.

"It does at the Plaza!"

"Girls, hurry! Wait till you see this" Nat says in a whistling tone.

"Our view from the terrace. It's to die for!"

"Holy, moly this is too good to be true!" Bekka bellows out.

"Yes, it is," Liv agrees.

"Who would have ever thought we'd be here tonight. It sure won't take long to get used to the good life. Our landscape has changed, ladies! I'm going to make use of our butler, Max and order a bottle of champagne. We'll celebrate beneath the twinkling stars looking at the captivating view of the park. What more could we ask for?" Liv spins around and spreads the luxurious drapes apart that cover the French doors. She re-enters the suite and spins in circles like a ballerina towards the end table until she reaches the phone.

"Good evening, Max."

"Good evening, Madame. How may I help you?"

"I would like to order a bottle of Dom Perignon and a bowl of strawberries with creme fraiche on the side," Liv requests, trying to curb her enthusiasm.

"Yes, of course, Madame. Right away."

"Merci!"

"Vous êtes le bienvenu," Max said.

"I guess that means you're welcome in French," Olivia whispers.

"Ladies, the Dom is on its way and we should really consider taking some French lessons. It's a sophisticated language and a sexy one!. Soon we'll have time and money to do whatever we want!"

"Time, huh! Do you really think we'll have more time on our hands? Managing all this money! It could rule our lives," Bekka states.

"A ring" interrupts them.

The sound makes them relish the moment with smug smiles.

"Well, I guess if you don't have a good plan it could. There are financial advisors you know. They handle it all." Liv yells out as she skips down the hallway admiring the gold furnishings and artwork.

"Yes, but who could you trust? Remember the Madoff scam? Those poor people lost everything. Their lives are ruined!" Bekka yelps.

"Bonsoir Madame. My name is Max. It is my pleasure to serve you."

"Welcome Max. It's nice to meet you."

"Where would you like me to leave the cart Madame?"

"The terrace, please. We're going to enjoy the breathtaking view."

"Sure thing." Max nods politely and smiles as he pushes the cart down the hall. As he moves through the grand living area, he silently admires the colossal chandelier. It's so exquisite he thinks.

"Bonsoir Mesdames."

"Good evening" Bekka and Nat greet Max simultaneously.

"I'll set everything over here. It will be my pleasure to open the champagne and serve you."

"That would be perfect, thank you!" Liv responds as she slips out onto the terrace.

Max fills the crystal champagne flutes and sets them on the silver tray next to the berries. "There you go ladies. Cheers!"

"Thank you, thank you, thank you" say the girls.

"You are so welcome. The pleasure is all mine. Don't hesitate to call if you need anything. I will let myself out, Madames. Bonne nuit!"

"Bonne nuit!" Nat replies.

"He is saying good night," Bekka says.

"Yes," informs Liv.

"Being fluent in a couple of languages certainly has its advantages."

"It sure does," agrees Bekka.

"Ladies let's make a toast" Nat raises her glass smiling.

"To us, our fortuitous evening, our future, our friendship, health and happiness, cheers!"

"Cheers!" they repeat.

"Wow, this is delish!" Liv giggles

"Yes, it is. We may need a second bottle," suggests Nat.

"Or, we can hold off until tomorrow. It's three hundred and ninety-five dollars a bottle" Bekka divulges.

"Who cares! The sky's the limit ladies! We deserve this! Unknowingly, we've been preparing for this evening all our lives," Nat declares.

"I agree! Now, let's make use of our sound system and listen to some tunes. We can dance and smoke a doobie. I happen to have one in my handbag" says Bekka, jovially.

"Absolutely, I need some music. I'm on it!" Liv says, spinning herself around and pausing to stare up at the blissful stars. She takes a deep breath, inhales the fresh air, savoring the moment. Her eyes roam across the canopy of the evening sky. She stares at the top of some of the most beautiful architecturally designed landmarked, Fifth Avenue buildings. Her eyes continued to wander down the windows and along the exquisite detail that each one bestows. She takes it all in, right down to the sidewalk where New Yorkers are prowling the streets.

Liv pounces into the room, kicks off her shoes, skips over to the built-in sound system and turns it on. "Sex is on Fire" by Kings of Leon is playing. She sings out loud as she grabs Bekka's purse and strolls out to the terrace.

"Here you go!" swinging the bag in Bekka's direction.

"Thanks doll!"

"I need to use the bathroom," Nat announces.

"I'll be right back.

In the meantime, feel free to go through my bag and find the doobie and a lighter."

"Sure thing," Liv assures her.

Nat enters one of the two colossal bathrooms. She stands there observing the regal fixtures and everything right down to the gilded door-knob. The jacuzzi is the largest she's ever seen. She lifts her dress and sits on the toilet. Her eyes wander from one end of the room to the other as she admires all of its details and the cascading chandelier hanging over the vanity. It sparkled like a Graff diamond. It's the most beautiful bathroom she has ever been in.

"Jesus what took you so long Nat? Did you get sick or something?" Bekka questions.

"Not at all! Ha-ha" Nat laughs.

"Just admiring the beauty of the place. I could have stayed in that bathroom the rest of the evening. It's unbelievable! It's the most beautiful one I've ever seen. I just had to take it all in. The details are exquisite and the jacuzzi is ginormous! You couldn't make it up in your dreams. Trust me!"

"Well, the whole place is over the top! I wouldn't expect anything less than extraordinariness. Here Nat, take a puff and catch up to us. We're feeling really good at the moment and haven't stopped laughing our asses off," Bekka states.

"Pass it along."

Nat takes a long drag and then exhales. As the music blares in the background, Bekka and Liv start dancing around the terrace. They spent the next few hours intermittently dancing, laughing and imbibing champagne. They laughed so hard they cried, embracing every moment.

The clock read 2 am, when the munchies started creeping up. Nat immediately called Max and ordered a few desserts off the menu.

"We'll take one Pots de crème, a Creme Brule, a chocolate strawberry platter and a key lime souffle."

"Will there be anything else Madame?" Max asks.

"Yes, another bottle of champagne and a bottle of sparkling water, please. Thank you very much," Nat says cheerfully as she places the phone down.

"How about a barf bag!" Bekka yells out as she moves to the beat of the music.

"I just checked out the bathrooms and you were right. The one with the jacuzzi is the bomb. Prrrretty fucking amazing! I've never seen anything like it," Liv expresses.

"Well then, let's road test the jacuzzi" Nat suggests.

"I'm in!" Bekka says, lifting the joint to her lips.

"Me too!" Liv complies.

"Now girls, we should plan a weekend trip to South Beach before the holidays. We can stay at the Delano Hotel in a suite overlooking the infinity pool just like we've always dreamed about," laughs Liv.

"Good idea, Liv! I like your thinking," Bekka responds with excitement

"Sounds good to me! You know how much I like South Beach," says Nat. "Isn't it nice, girls, that we can afford to do anything, anything our hearts desire?"

"How sweet it is" shouts Bekka as she dances down the hall, twirling herself around.

Nat and Liv imitate her, and one by one they enter the bathroom like three ballerinas.

"This is really incredible. Look at the selection of bath gels. What are you in the mood for? We have lavender, verbena, vanilla, gardenia and rose. They all sound delicious" states Liv.

"This whole evening is incredible. I'm still pinching myself expecting to wake up from a dream. I like lavender" Bekka murmurs.

"I don't want this weekend to end! I don't want it to end!" cries out Nat.

"Me either!" Says Liv.

"Me three! Should we mix the lavender and verbena together?" suggests Bekka.

"Works for me!" says Liv as she turns the gold ornate faucet handles.

"Look at this! There are robes, slippers and silk nighties hanging in the closet. Just for us. They're all La Perla. My favorite!" Bekka squeals.

"You mean Ted's favorite, right B?" comments Liv.

Bekka and Nat giggle as they pull everything out of the closet.

"They're all so luxurious. Which one do you like, Liv? One has an animal print and the others are solid with lace trim?" Nat points out.

"Doesn't matter to me, they're all gorgeous. I'm sure they all feel good."

Nat and Liv undress and step into the intoxicating bath water. They relax and observe Bekka holding up a negligee and admiring herself in the mirror. Nat laughs out loud. "B, you're cracking me up! You look like you've never seen anything so beautiful in your life. For god's sake come join us."

"I have a nice buzz on. Try not to kill it. I'm coming! I'm coming!" Bekka shouts.

Liv hits the remote, turns up the music, and lights three large aromatherapy candles sitting on the ledge of the jacuzzi.

"It doesn't get better than this" Liv yells out as Bekka hurls one leg over the tub.

Bekka lifts her other leg, and slips, losing her balance. She falls hard into the jacuzzi nearly hitting her head on the ledge. Her plunge creates a mini tidal wave and water hits Nat and Liv in the face. The water rises over their heads and lands on the bathroom floor.

Bekka lifts her head out of the water. They all look at each other, and laugh. Liv could hardly catch her breath until she heard a knock at the door.

"Shoot! We forgot we ordered room service," shouts Liv.

"No, you forgot you ordered room service," says Bekka as she glances over at Nat.

"Or maybe they're here because we flooded the floor beneath us," Liv replies, roaring with laughter.

"Stay put girls, I'll get it," Nat says as she gains her balance and stands up. She tosses a bath towel on the floor to soak up the sudsy water, steps out of the tub, throws on a robe and a pair of slippers and exits the bathroom.

A couple of minutes later she enters the bathroom with a mini silver serving cart. It has a cascading tower of sweets, champagne and water on ice, three crystal glasses, the finest china and a fishbowl vase with peonies.

"Girls look at this!" Nat says as she parks the cart next to the jacuzzi. "I'm going to serve you so stay put she commands as she bites into a chocolate covered strawberry."

"Yum! OMG! Wait until you taste this! So delicious!" she confirms. "Everything looks incredible!" Liv says moving her body forward to have full visibility of the cart.

"There has to be five thousand calories on that cart," speculates Bekka.

"Well, there's no time like the present, to overindulge. We should make a rule not to count anything this weekend. Not pounds, calories, money, hours of shopping, missed gym time, phone calls, emails, nothing! Nothing! Nothing at all!" states Nat as she pours the champagne into the flutes.

"Well, I'll toast to that. Cheers!" Liv says as they raise their glasses and toast.

"Our landscape has changed. This weekend we live life as we are, three little rich girls in the big apple with freedom to do whatever our hearts desire. We've earned this, girls! But we must be mindful. It's important that it doesn't change who we are."

"I'm sure we'll change a few things in our lives just because we can but let's not forget we are happy, privileged and blessed women before this evening happened. This is the cherry on the cake! Happiness is a state of mind. Being happy with yourself is paramount! Now, we can enrich the lives of others, people we love and people who are less fortunate," Liv expresses in an enthusiastic tone.

"Yes, I agree. We must keep our eye on the ball," agrees Bekka. "Having financial freedom gives you the advantage to make decisions and take risks. I have a lot to consider now. My marriage, my relationship with Ted, my children, their future, my future and so on. The truth is I am so in love with Ted and I don't want to be. I try to talk myself out of it when we're apart. I tell myself it's not the right thing and I need to end it.

"Then we see each other, and I feel so connected to him. I know he feels the same. The chemistry is there. He brings out the best in me. Part of me says fuck it, we only live once. I often wonder about Larry. If he is living a secret life. His behavior is inconsistent, and we don't communicate as much as we should. My gut tells me he is pursuing other women. He sucks most days. He's a selfish idiot and disrespectful.

"I will always love him because of our twenty-year history and our children but I don't always like him. I loathe him most of the time. I've been fearful of walking away before Ted entered my life. Didn't want to get blamed for breaking up the family and upheaving our lives. But now, things are different. I could live my truth and be happy ever after. I deserve it!"

Nat, wide eyed, says, "Wow, girl that was a lot to divulge. Of course, you do deserve the best. We all do!"

"Yes, we do! It's my turn, girls" Liv chimes in. "I feel your pain, B. Sometimes, I fantasize about being with another man. Jack no longer tells me I look beautiful. It's gotten to the point we're I'll ask him if I look good in something. He'll glance at me and then respond, 'you always look good, Liv'.

They just don't get it!

"We love being told we look beautiful and receiving a bouquet of flowers when we don't expect to. Women need to feel good, respected and acknowledged. He's been so inconsistent, that I no longer expect it. Maybe it's normal that distance comes between two people after so many years of marriage. I don't know.

"We all get caught up with the responsibility of raising a family, working and life. It's a lot of juggling and a lot of pressure. It sucks you in. We try to balance everything, but something is always compromised. Jack is a hustler and has always been financially responsible. It wouldn't surprise me if he was glaring at our mortgage balance right now.

"The truth is no one is perfect. We're only human. All my married friends complain about their marital issues and my single friends complain about not finding someone to marry. It all comes down to having the courage to make changes, make decisions, find your balance and live."

"True. Very true. It certainly comes down to balance," replies Bekka.

"In a nutshell, the two of you put marriage in perspective for me. Maybe I should start cherishing every moment of singlehood," says Nat.

"Yes, take some of the pressure off yourself, Nat. I guarantee you'll meet someone who really loves you for you. And now that you have financial independence you don't need to settle or look for someone who can offer you a certain lifestyle. You're living your reality, right now!" Bekka roars.

"Yes, we all are! On a separate note, I really miss my girls. I never go to bed without hugging and kissing them. I'm having withdrawals," mentions Liv.

"Me too," Bekka chimes in. "Chad and Addy are definitely going to wonder where I am when they wake. They'll think Larry and I had a fight.

We always make breakfast together on Sundays. Hopefully Larry won't disappoint them. What can I say, men are unpredictable."

"I would like another glass of bubbly. Can someone pass the champagne?" Liv requests holding up her glass.

"Well, girls I know, no marriage is perfect," retorts Nat as she refills the flutes. "But, I am in my mid-thirties and I just want to know that there is a Mr. Right out there. My biological clock is ticking and now I have choices. I don't have to wait any longer! I can start the infertility treatments immediately and raise children on my own.

"I am so over the moon by the thought of it. Whatever happens, happens! Dating is exhausting and gets daunting at times. Everyone has so much baggage. At this point, I want to cross all the men off my list and start with a clean slate. Be independent and in some sort of control. Except Jacob! I'll keep him around. He's amazing! He gives me his undivided attention and support. A born caretaker."

"His hearing comes through caring. All the other men have selective hearing" Bekka giggles.

"Don't we know it?" Liv states smiling. The three of them look at each other and laugh.

"We better change the subject. This could get toxic plus the water is cooling down. Should we think about getting some shut eye girls? We have a big day tomorrow" prompts Liv.

"Yes, we should," Bekka agrees as she stands up slowly to exit the bathwater.

"Nat, I've been meaning to ask you, what was all the laughter we overheard earlier when you answered the door?"

Nat giggles. "Ha, I was just about to fill the two of you in. Max's shift ended and-"

"Who is Max?" Bekka asks.

"Our butler."

"Oh, right," responds Bekka.

"We have a new butler. His name is Phoenix. Phoenix Harley from Dallas Texas. A real looker. He's in his early thirties. Claims he is an actor. Works here part time for extra cash. He started flirting with me and he made me laugh. I flirted back" says Nat smiling. "He asked how long I was staying at the hotel."

"Not surprised, in the least bit. I would flirt with you too. You're gorgeous! Plus, you answered the door in a silk robe. You flirted with his imagination" adds Bekka.

"Ha, right! He informed me he's working 'til ten this morning and will return tomorrow evening at six. I invited him to stop by so you can meet him. He's a little young, but a hunk," Nat giggles as they each slip on a silk nightgown and a pair of velour slippers monogrammed with The Plaza logo.

They brush their teeth at the gilded marble vanity before jumping into bed.

"OMG, these beds are incredible! I feel like I'm sleeping on a cloud" Liv expresses as she stretches her body across and hugs a pillow.

"Yes, and they're ginormous. I don't think Bekka and I will come close to touching each other," giggles Nat.

"Well, I guess it depends on whether or not you do cartwheels in your sleep," Bekka laughs. When my kids sleep with me, they flip and flop all night long and I end up at the end of the bed with someone's feet in my face."

"I'm familiar with that," giggles Liv.

"Well nightie, night girls. Love you," shouts out Bekka over the blaring sirens echoing down Fifth Avenue.

"Love you too. Sweet dreams!" Liv and Nat squeak out simultaneously.

"Are we really going to sleep, girls?" Bekka asks in a sleepy tone just before dozing off.

"EAT, SHOP & BE MILLIONAIRES"

Liv's internal clock wakes her the following morning. She's the first to rise and strolls quietly into the bathroom rubbing her eyes. Perusing her surroundings, she smiles gently, reflecting back on the evening's festivities. She can't believe it's not a dream. Glancing at the big gold Cartier clock on the vanity she stretches her arms over her head, letting out a big yawn.

Wow, it's nine forty-five. I actually slept well, considering the amount of champagne we consumed. My eyes look good, not too puffy she thinks as she examines them in the mirror. Liv exits the bathroom, heads towards the terrace and gingerly opens the doors. The light buzz of the city fills the air.

She steps outside and walks to the railing to admire the Sunday morning view. She takes a deep breath in and then exhales. She is shiftless as she admires the treetops that fill Central Park with precision. Her eyes are drawn downward to the well-dressed churchgoers tapping along the street towards St. Patrick's church.

"Good Morning Liv" Nat whispers as she enters the terrace. "Did you sleep well?"

"Wonderfully. It's a miracle I don't have a hangover. You?"

Nat laughs. "I feel pretty good. I slept like a baby. I don't think that's the case for Bekka. She started mumbling something about a migraine the minute she woke up and headed straight for the bathroom."

"That sucks! Do we have any Tylenol, or should I call and request some before she starts bitchin?"

"No need" giggles Nat. "It's in the complimentary toiletry bag. I took some last night before bed."

"Smart! Let's make sure she stays hydrated, and eats something asap!"

"That wouldn't hurt any of us," adds Nat.

"We'll feel better once we start shopping."

"Morning," Bekka said in a groggy tone as she stepped out on the terrace."

"Good Morning to you" Liv and Nat respond giggling.

Confused, Bekka asks, "What's so funny? Come on, share. It's no surprise but I have a migraine. I just took Tylenol."

"Well, for one, your nightgown is on backwards. I guess we were either too fucked up or in the moment not to notice it last night," Nat chimes in.

Liv continues in a giggly tone. "Two, your hair looks like a bird's nest, and three, you only have one slipper on."

They all laugh. Liv tries to catch her breath as she and Nat stare at Bekka, watching her pat her hair down.

"Drink some water so you can shake off the pain," Liv suggests as she continues laughing and passes a glass of water almost spilling it.

"Thanks! My right foot is killing me. I may have sprained it when I fell last night. I just ordered a pair of ballet flats from BG. They're going to be delivered in fifteen minutes. There's no way I'm strutting the city in anything higher. To top it off, my Amex card was declined. Larry hasn't paid the bill. It's three weeks past due. Why couldn't this happen to him, when he's out to dinner?!"

"Hmm, don't let it upset you." suggests Nat.

"I had to call Amex and answer two fucking security questions to get the charge approved. It intensified my headache."

Liv and Nat hold back until Bekka finishes before they all start laughing. Once they calmed down, they took notice of the activity below. The horse and carriages, taxis and limos were in full swing circling Grand Army Plaza making pit stops at the entrance of the hotel.

"It's so nice to wake up in the city, girls. I haven't done it since I lived here. Fifteen years at least."

"Yes, it is," agrees Bekka.

"I think it's one of my reasons for going into real estate. My office will be on the upper west side. It's a lovely neighborhood and right near the park. The big apple has always been my favorite city."

"So, you're still planning on working?" Nat inquires.

"Yes, doll, that's the plan. When have you known me to do anything other than what I say I'm going to do?"

Nat stares at Liv.

"I'll just have more aggressive goals due to the fortunate circumstances and I'll work when I want to," smiles Liv. "Plus, I'll have my finger on the pulse. It will give me intel on what's happening in the market. It's an advantage for all of us. Maybe we'll buy some investment properties, ladies. Who knows what the future holds? We have the world by the balls, remember?"

"True, true. Well then, stick to your plan! I would love to get a place in the city to stay with the kids on weekends. Especially during the holiday rush. They love the city. We spend a lot of time here and it would be such an experience for them," adds Bekka.

"As for me, I should stop wasting my money on rent and buy a nice loft in Soho or Tribeca" chuckles Nat. "Liv, I think you are looking at your first client."

"Great!" Liv laughs.

"Girls, I just texted Jaxon. He's available to drive us around. Should we get ready and head down to the Palm Court for breakfast?"

"Good thinking, Liv! It sounds perfect. Let's do it!" says Nat.

"I hear a knock at the door. My shoes are here!" Sings Bekka.

"I'm going to jump in the shower and then call the girls before we head out. I'm sure they're up and asking for me," expresses Liv.

"Yes, I miss mine too. Chad and Addy already texted me. They're wondering where I am and when I'm coming home."

Liv dries herself as she walks into the room, overhearing the tail end of Bekka's phone conversation.

"Don't worry mommy will be home tomorrow. I'll be there by the time you get home from school. I'll take you for ice cream. I promise! Be good for Nana and daddy today. No fighting. I miss you and love you. Call you later. Bye-bye."

Liv dresses quickly in the same dress, and heels she wore the night before as she dials her daughters. She was craving a new outfit and a pair of comfortable shoes.

"Hello Bea, it's Mama. Good morning, sweetie. Did I wake you?"

"No, Mama. Me and Juliet are getting ready for religion. Daddy is going to take us. When are you coming home? We all miss you. Tito and Daisy too. Tito is running circles around the house. I love you mama."

"I know, sweetie. I'll be home tomorrow afternoon. I miss and love you too! Enjoy religion and have fun with Nonno. I'll call you before bedtime."

"Okay, love you too. Can I speak to your sisters?"

"Hi Mom. Are you okay?" Nikki asks.

"Yes, sweetie. I just decided to spend the weekend in the city with Bekka and Nat. We're celebrating."

"Whose birthday is it?" asks Nikki.

"No one's birthday. We're just celebrating something. It's a surprise! I'll tell you all about it tomorrow when I get home. I promise! I love you and I'll speak to you later. Mwah!"

"Love you too mom. Have fun. Here's Jules."

"Mom, I miss you so much. Please come home."

"I know sweetie, I miss you too. Mama will be home before you know it! Enjoy your day with Nonno. It's beautiful out! Ask him to take you all to the park. I'm sure some of your friends will be there."

"Okay Mom, but I really need your help with my science project. It's due on Thursday. We'll have to work on it tomorrow. Love you."

"We absolutely will! I love you. Any chance daddy is around?"

"He's in the shower, mom. He's leaving for work soon. I'll tell him you called."

"Okay, thanks sweetie. Love you so much. Bye-Bye."

Liv sat quietly for a moment. A feeling of emptiness arose as she thought about how much she misses her daughters.

"Liv, are you ready?" asks Nat, interrupting her thoughts.

"Almost. Just need to fix my hair and brush my teeth. Give me five, please."

"I need a few more minutes too," Bekka chimes in.

"Okay. Come find me on the terrace when you're both ready. After all, how often do we get to wake up in a place with a view like this? It's so amazing. I feel amazing! The whole weekend is amazing!" Nat says jovially.

"Yes, it really is too perfect to be true" Liv agrees.

A few minutes later, Bekka dances out onto the balcony twirling around. "Look girls, they fit like a glove."

"They look very comfortable. I'm ready when you are!" Nat informs.

"How about you, Liv?"

Liv doesn't answer.

"Hey, girlfriend, what's the matter? You okay?"

"Yes. Just thinking about my girls. I miss them a lot. I want to buy them something at FAO Schwartz. You know I'm seldom away from them. Why don't you girls get a jump start on shopping after breakfast. I'll meet you at Bergdorf's. Keep your eyes out for a couple of outfits and comfortable shoes to get me through the weekend. You know my taste."

"We will," Nat replies.

"I can't wait to get out of these clothes! I feel like a dirty stay out. It brings back memories of the days I lived in the city and never made it home" giggles Liv.

"Yeah, I bet it does! Now, let's go and eat!" Nat says as she struts down the hallway. Liv and Bekka follow suit to the elevator. They enter the dining room as if they've been there a dozen times.

"Good Morning. How many, ladies?" Asks the attractive five-foot ten hostess with eyelash extensions.

"Three please," Bekka replies.

"Right this way." The hostess leads them to a table at the far end of the restaurant. The perfect spot to take in a panoramic view of the room.

"The palm trees add such a nice feeling to the place. Don't you think girls?" inquires Nat.

"Yes, it's just gorgeous. I haven't eaten here in a long time. I enjoyed Thanksgiving here one year with some colleagues when I lived on the upper east side. We had such a blast," smiles Liv reflecting back.

"What a classy place and everything on the menu sounds so delicious. It's tough to choose. Hmm, I think I'm going with the eggs Florentine," says Bekka.

"I will have the same," Nat adds.

"I'm going with the oatmeal and berries. My norm. I don't want to eat anything that could disrupt my day. My stomach is sensitive. I'd even love to grab a green juice somewhere." Liv states.

"It's so lovely here. The flowers are aromatic. The place is very regal, and the service is impeccable. Everything is so alluring. Look at us! We're like three princesses," Bekka smiles as breakfast is placed in front of them.

"We're not like princesses, we are princesses!" announces Liv, as she spoons oatmeal into her mouth.

"Girls, I'm feeling quite full already. I ate too much last night. Let's finish up so we can go shop our hearts out," smiles Nat as she raises her coffee cup.

"I'm ready! Let's do it!" Bekka shouts out as she signals the waiter for the check. "I'm going to head out now, girls and get a head start. I shouldn't be more than thirty minutes. I'll text you when I'm on my way. Have fun!"

"You too!"

Liv crosses Fifth Avenue with a bounce in her step. She observes the crowd of tourists with cameras loitering outside the shop.

Liv enters the store. She chooses a thoughtful gift for each of her daughters, a Wii sporting game for Jack and a couple of chew toys for Tito and Daisy. She heads to the checkout area where long lines await her. She texts Jaxon to arrange the pick-up and delivery to Brooklyn.

"Yes, it would be great if you could gift wrap everything and send it over to the Plaza. Thanks so much!" Liv hastily signs the receipt, weaves herself through the crowded shop and exits. She texts Bekka and Nat.

Nat replies- *We're in designer shoes, second floor. It will be easy to find us. We're sitting next to Daffy Duck. You can't miss her! Lol.*

Liv giggles as she spins through the revolving door and heads towards the elevator.

She enters the shoe department like a kid in a candy store. She easily spots a very disfigured faced woman, where Nat and Bekka are sitting.

"Hey girls, having fun yet?"

"Yes, I feel like I'm high," Bekka toots.

"They have the most amazing collection of shoes and boots."

"I can see that. I'm going to try a few myself," squeals Liv.

One hour and forty-eight hundred dollars later they exit the shoe department and travel to contemporary clothing on the third floor. They purchase a few things to cover themselves for the weekend then, head straight to the handbag department.

"I'll take this one!" Bekka and Nat overhear Liv, as she admires herself in the mirror with a crocodile handbag slung over her shoulder.

"Wow, that's so gorgeous," Nat blurts out.

"Yes, it's gorgeous and I love it! I always wanted a crocodile bag."

"I bet Jack would have bought it for you if you asked for it," states Bekka. "He's so generous. Larry, on the other hand, is frugal and talks his way out of buying me expensive everything. One year he bought me a faux Chanel tote on the corner of fifty seventh street. Naturally, it took me thirty seconds to identify it was fake.

"The bag had a funny odor and the lining didn't have the 'double C' logo on it. I said, 'Nice try, Lar!' His response was 'Hun, you may know it's a fake but no one else will.'

"Just to prove him wrong, I started wearing it to the office and three weeks later the bag started to peel and one of the straps broke. I insisted on carrying it around until he bought me a real one. Eventually, he broke down and purchased a second hand one that was gingerly used."

They all laugh.

"Doll, now you can buy whatever you want. Isn't that wonderful? We can buy it for ourselves. Whatever our hearts desire. Who needs a man?!" blasts Nat.

"Yes, that's true but either way we need to keep it all in perspective. Every day will not be like this. We have to be sensible! We shouldn't be compulsive because we can afford to be. We never want to look like that woman in the shoe department. The poor thing is ruined and there's no turning back. A sure sign of insecurity. She's terribly disfigured and all she wants to be is beautiful. Spending mindfully should be a rule of thumb" Liv retorts in a soft tone.

"I agree, but let's apply that rule after the weekend. I'm definitely investing in some Botox in the near future. I hate the creases in my forehead, and I heard that stuff performs miracles. I promise not to go overboard. Promise!" declares Bekka. Nat rolled her eyes at Bekka.

"So, girls, it's almost two o'clock. Our purchases will be delivered to the hotel. What do you say? Do we take a break from retail therapy and grab some chow?" Liv suggests.

"Do we have to? This kind of therapy is so much fun!" giggles Bekka. Although, I'll admit I am a little hungry. Why don't we grab lunch at Cipriani's?"

"If you don't mind, I prefer something on the healthier side. Can we go somewhere else? Nat asks.

"Yes, I agree. Plus, their food is decadent, and it may make us sick after last night's indulgences," comments Liv.

"Two against one! Where to, girls?" Bekka asks.

"How about Milos? It's a few blocks away. The fish is so fresh and delicious. I'll text Jaxon and tell him to meet us there. He should be heading back from Brooklyn by now." Liv says as her phone rings.

"Sounds good. Let's go!" Nat and Bekka agree.

"Hey Jack, what's going on?"

"What's going on with you? Some shopping, I see. We just got a shit load of gifts. The girls are so happy. Where are you?"

"We're on our way to Milos for lunch."

"Good. I know how much you like that place. We haven't been there in years. I remember how much you love their martini's. Just take it easy. The last time we were there I practically carried you out," laughs Jack.

"Not to worry, Jack. We imbibed so much champagne last night. It's a miracle that I feel as good as I do. Maybe rich people don't get hang-overs, Jack!"

"Ha, don't kid yourself. Having money can cause lots of problems and you know it. How many stories have we heard about people losing everything because of greed?"

"Too many. I remember them. Some are devastating."

"Hey, what time are you heading to work?"

"Soon. My father just got here. The girls are in good hands. Give them a call in a couple of hours and check in."

"Will do! Speak to you later Jack. Don't work too hard. Bye."

"Bye Liv, have fun!"

They walk briskly to the restaurant laughing every step of the way.

"This restaurant is amazing! Love this place and everyone looks normal," chuckles Bekka. "I think I'm going to have the lobster salad."

"The upper east-side has always been an interesting place. Plastic surgery and shopping are careers for some women. They're overcompensating for some void in their lives. It's sad. They're starving for attention. I'm going with the grilled Branzino" adds Liv.

"Hmm, that's probably true. I'm going with the lobster salad too," says Nat.

"Like I said, girls being mindful plays a big part in the next chapter of our lives," Liv reiterates.

"Yes, it certainly does," agrees Bekka.

"You know one of my biggest fears is to end up worse off than where I started. It happens to so many people. Most of them become homeless or have to move back home with their parents" Liv informs.

"Ha, well that won't happen to us! Don't be paranoid. You're too smart. You have worked too hard to get where you are" Nat chimes in.

"You're right! I'm overthinking everything at the moment. Making the right decisions for my daughters is at the forefront of my mind."

"Well, my biggest fear is becoming a serial-dater and never finding Mr. Right," giggles Nat.

"Mr. Right will happen when you're not looking. Trust me, that's how everything happens. When you don't expect it. Just like winning the lottery," smiles Bekka.

"Wow, the food is so delicious" states Liv.

"It's so fresh," says Nat as she pokes at her lobster salad.

"The difference is now you have options. You can do everything on your own with or without a man. How good does that feel? You can be a single mom if you choose. Marriage isn't a must like it was for our parents. Couples have children out of wedlock. It's quite the norm today. It's exciting to know that nothing will hold you back. Isn't it? After all, Bekka and I can't wait to be a godmother. Maybe, you'll have twins like us. We should rub elbows and make a wish."

They laugh.

"You're funny, Liv. I would love to have twins. The thought of it excites me so much. What's the post lunch plan?

"Jaxon will be here in fifteen minutes. What should we do next, girls?" asks Liv.

"Smart planning on your part to have Jaxon drive us, Liv. Why don't we hit the meatpacking district and do some shopping since we never made it there the other night," suggests Bekka.

"For good reason we never made it there. In that case, let's get the check," Liv says, as she waves her hand in the air to grab the waiter's attention.

"Whenever you're ready. Thank you, ladies," the waiter says as he places the check down.

"Thank you" Nat replies. "What a cutie!" she whispers in a low tone.

"Speaking of cuties, I hope I see Phoenix later on today."

"I'm sure you will. I really need to get a green juice," Liv mentions.

"Thanks again ladies and have a wonderful day," says the waiter.

"Same to you" they respond as they hit the ladies' room before exiting the restaurant.

They spot Jaxon waiting outside the front door.

"Perfect, there he is!" points out Bekka.

"Hello, Jaxon. Nice to see you," greets Liv.

"Hello, ladies. How's your day going?" he asks.

"Fucking fabulous!"

"Incredible!"

"It's amazing!"

They respond simultaneously and start laughing along with Jaxon.

"Wonderful! I'm glad to hear it ladies. Where are we headed?"

"To the meatpacking district please. We need a few more hours of retail therapy and then onto happy hour," Nat informs.

"You got it! By the way, Mrs. Sardi, everything was delivered to Brooklyn. Your daughters are very sweet."

"Thanks, so much Jaxon! It's so appreciated. I would have loved to see their expressions."

"They're beauties, I must tell you. You are very blessed, madam."

"Please, call me Liv."

"Will do, Liv," Jaxon replies as he exits the highway.

"You can let us out on the corner on ninth, thank you," requests Bekka.

"Okay ladies, here you go! Send me a text ten minutes prior to pick up."

"Will do thanks," Nat replies as she shifts her body toward the car door.

"Have fun, ladies. See you soon."

"Ciao!" says Bekka.

"Listen to you," laughs Nat.

"What can I say? I am having an Italian moment."

"It's probably the only word you know," teases Nat.

"That may be true, but now I can take lessons, and learn to speak the language fluently," Bekka states, twirling around on the street corner waiting for the light to change.

"That's for sure. Hey girls, let's hit some of the designer boutiques. Look B, La Perla is across the street," Liv points out.

"Let's do it!" Nat says enthusiastically.

Two hours later.....

"I'm spent. Retail therapy is exhausting," says Bekka as she looks down at several shopping bags and smirks.

"It sure is! I need a pick-me-up. Let's grab a cocktail!" suggests Liv.

"Sounds good. I feel pretty good and I'd love a cocktail!" chimes in Nat.

"Of course, you feel good. You're twelve years younger than us, and have a lot less stress," laughs Bekka.

"I have stress, it's just different than yours," Nat states.

"Jaxon will be pulling up in a minute, girls to take our bags.

The place on the corner looks pretty lively. Maybe we should give it a try," Liv suggests as she observes the crowd.

"Sure," Nat and Bekka respond as Jaxon pulls up.

"Hi ladies."

He smiles as he loads the bags in the trunk. "Looks like the meat-packing district was a hit for you ladies."

"Yes, it sure was. Retail therapy is hard work," giggles Nat. "Now we need a cocktail. We're heading to the bar across the street."

"Take your time ladies. Enjoy yourselves," Jaxon replies.

"See you soon!" yells Bekka.

They elbow their way through the crowd towards the large oak bar.

"Hi ladies. What can I get you?" the bartender asks.

"Three Belvedere martinis, a little dirty, straight up with olives. Thank you," Liv screams out over the music.

"Coming right up!"

They observe the pretty crowd, waiting for drinks, getting shoved, in all different directions.

"This place is jammed! I feel like I'm on the subway during rush hour," yells out Nat.

"Yes, it does feel that way," agrees Bekka.

"Here you go ladies. Cheers!" says the bartender as he places their drinks in front of them.

"Thank you," says Liv. "To us girls!"

"Cheers," Nat and Bekka yell simultaneously.

"Yum, this is one good martini. I feel buzzed already" says Bekka.

"Of course, you do. You practically sucked it down," says Nat.

"We need to think about eating something. It's nearly seven o'clock. We should head back to the hotel soon. We can order room service or grab something from the food hall on the lower level. I would like to call my girls before bedtime," states Liv.

"That works for me! I need to call mine too," agrees Bekka.

"Fine with me," Nat says as she twirls a strand of her hair around her finger.

"Let's do a shot before we go!"

"You're an instigator, Bekka. You really want to be sick, again don't you?" inquires Nat.

"I'm not going to be sick. Besides, I already ordered three shots of tequila and they're sitting on the bar."

"Girls night out!" Liv toasts as she raises her glass.

"Cheers! Happy days to come!" announces Nat.

"I'll drink to that!" Bekka says sucking down the shot.

"I'm going to text Jaxon. My stomach is churning. I need some chow soon" Liv states.

"Please don't turn into a grump," states Bekka.

"Me, never? You must be talking about yourself. You're the one who gets bossy after a few drinks."

"Girls, girls, let's not get bitchy now," Nat insists.

"We're not. We're just behaving like sisters."

"Yes, twisted sisters," giggles Liv.

"Jaxon is parked across the street. Are we ready to head out ladies?" asks Liv.

"Sure, Let's go!" replies Nat.

"I feel good," Bekka shouts out as she dances her way towards the door.

Liv and Nat trail behind laughing as they watch Bekka shake her booty.

"We have the whole night ahead of us girls and it's going to be fun. After all, tomorrow night we'll be missing one another. I'll be alone in my tiny upper east side apartment counting millions."

"Of course we will miss each other," says Bekka. "But there will be more weekends like this."

"Of course. We should plan a weekend to South Beach for Bekka's birthday in December" Liv whispers to Nat.

"That's a great idea! I'll book it this week. We'll surprise her. I smell the lavender bushes and lemon trees already. I'm dreaming of us laying on a ginormous white, fluffy chaise lounge drinking cosmos," giggles Nat.

"I am taking my real estate exam after Thanksgiving, so the timing is perfect," remarks Liv.

"That's what's his name," says Bekka as she points across the street at the SUV.

"You mean Jaxon?" asks Nat.

"Yeah, yeah. I forgot his name."

"Feeling good, doll?"

"Yes, Nat. I feel really good," Bekka replies, sliding into the car.

"Hey Jaxon, we're going to the hotel for the night,"assures Liv.

"You got it ladies! I hope you enjoyed your day."

"We did! We definitely did! Now all I need is a bubble bath and some room service," slurs Bekka.

"That sounds good. I'm beat. We'll hang out on the terrace and chill. After all, tomorrow is Monday, our big day. We pick up our winnings, girls! I still can't believe I'm saying this. The location is somewhere downtown. At the moment, I can't remember where" comments Liv.

"No worries. I'll look it up when we get back to the hotel," Nat offers.

Feeling exhausted, they sit quietly staring out the window on the ride back.

"Good night, ladies. It was a pleasure. See you tomorrow!"

"Good night Jaxon and thank you," Liv replies as she exits the car. She trails behind Bekka and Nat, up the red carpeted stairs, and one by one they disappear into the revolving doors, heading straight to the elevator.

"Madames, good evening. Many packages have been delivered to your room," Max informs them, as they continue down the colossal hallway.

"Merci", says Liv as she removes the room key from her shiny new crocodile handbag. They file into the room one by one and kick off their shoes.

"Let's order immediately. I'm famished" suggests Bekka.

"Go ahead, you do the honors. You know what we like," retorts Nat.

Bekka places their dinner order and then drifts through the French doors out to the terrace. "Aah finally," she says as she takes a seat next to the potted hydrangea plant.

"I'm exhausted. Did you call the girls, Liv? Larry just put Chad & Addie in bed and is reading them a bedtime story. I'm thrilled. It's been a long time since he's done either. It's good for him to get a taste of it."

"Yes, I just spoke to the girls. They were waiting for me to call. They're also in bed. They all sound exhausted. They had a fun day. My father-in-law is with them, and Jack's on his way home."

The doorbell rings.

"Sounds like the food is here," says Bekka .

A moment later Nat appears on the balcony with a tall handsome guy. "Girls, this is Phoenix."

"Hello ladies, nice to meet you."

Liv and Bekka turn and greet him as they give him a once over. Nat giggles as she witnesses it. Phoenix has large blue eyes, high cheekbones, full lips, a thick head of wavy blonde hair and a perfect 6'1 build that resembles JFK Jr's.

121

"You look like you just walked out of GQ magazine," blurts out Bekka. Then she follows up with "Can you stay a while?" in a raspy sexy voice.

"Not long," Phoenix says blushing. "I'm still on my shift. I get off at midnight."

"Well, stop by afterwards. Unless, you have other plans," inquires Nat.

"No, no plans. Are you sure you'll be up for it?"

"Yes, come by. It will be nice to have some testosterone around. We haven't had much interaction with men this weekend. We're husbandless. Well- Liv and I are," giggles Bekka.

"Sounds good ladies. By the way, your dinner is sitting pretty on a cart in the living room. Shall I move everything out here?"

"Yes, that would be perfect, Thank you!" replies Liv.

"Here you go ladies, enjoy! I'll see you all soon," Phoenix says, as he nestles the cart in a corner, on the terrace.

"Bye Phoenix. Thank you. Yes, thank you," Bekka and Liv both respond waving their hands in the air.

"I'll walk you out," Nat insists.

"Oh my God, if he's not the hottest thing I've ever seen standing next to you then I must be blind," Bekka roars as Nat returns onto the terrace.

"Ha, ha. Yes, he's a hottie. A bit young but very hot."

"You told us he was a cutie pie not a vision of perfection," adds Bekka.

"Well, I had to leave something out," giggles Nat.

"It will be fun later when he joins us."

"I'm sure it will be," adds Liv.

Bekka is excited at this point. "Girls let's dig in! I ordered your favorites. Baby lamb chops, roasted truffle mash potatoes, asparagus, Maine lobster mango salad, and sea bass with chanterelle mushrooms."

"Yum, sounds delish. Thanks, Bekka!" smiles Liv

"And girls, in addition we have caviar and a bottle of bubbly to wash it all down. We can order dessert later."

"We don't need dessert. We have Phoenix. Eye candy is a lot less calories," chuckles Liv.

"You mean she has Phoenix," mumbles Bekka as she feeds herself a forkful of lobster salad.

"True!" replies Liv.

"OMG, the lobster is to die for."

"So are the lamb chops," confirms Nat.

"This meal is mouthwatering," brags Liv.

Remind me, after dinner, to search the address of the lottery office so we can plan our morning. Plus, I need to let the Jew know I'm coming in late," says Nat as she dips a lamb chop in the mint jelly.

"Ha, you're actually going to work? You should totally quit! He's been taking you for granted for years. Start your own business, girl! Every time I visit his eyes are on your ass. Tell him the burglary traumatized you and that you have PTSD, or you met someone and moved back to Russia," laughs Bekka. "At least take a few days off, doll!"

"You're funny, B. Yes, I suppose you're right. I should take some time off. I'm just afraid I'll get bored without the two of you, and be compulsive with my winnings," says Nat.

"I understand, but you know that won't happen. Go to a day spa," suggests Liv.

"Good idea!"

"How about some caviar and more bubbly, girls?"

Liv pulls the champagne out of the ice bucket and refills the glasses.

"I've never been more ready," responds Bekka.

"Dig in!"

"Yum! It's like salted silk on your tongue," moans Liv.

"Boy, this stuff is good. I don't understand how people can say they hate caviar. Maybe, it's just the idea of eating fish eggs that's a turn off. I, on the other hand, can certainly get used to it."

"I've never tasted caviar quite like this, and I have it at least once a week, with one of the rich men," Nat mentions as she piles a lump of it on a blini.

"I'm starting to feel full, girls," states Bekka.

"Yes, me too. I'm going to excuse myself, take a short break to look up the address to the NYS Lottery Customer Service Center. I'll be right back," says Nat as she exits the terrace and walks swiftly to the gold leafed desk and takes a seat. She opens the laptop and taps at the keys to search the address.

"Ah, there it is," Nat mumbles to herself. She enters the info in her phone as she hears laughter in the background. "Girls, guess what?"

"What?" inquires Liv laughing with champagne drooling down her chin.

"They open at ten am! The place is on Beaver Street. Just downtown."

Bekka and Liv look at Nat and laugh loudly.

"What is?" Bekka snorts.

"The lottery customer service center. Did you forget already?"

"Not a chance!" Bekka yelps out.

"Well, that sounds easy peasy. We should order room service for morning," suggests Liv.

"Agree. Besides, it will be our last meal before we check out. The morning rush hour will be quite invigorating from the terrace. After all, we should enjoy the bird's eye view," adds Nat.

"It's all too good to be true," says Liv.

"So, ladies, do you want to know the total after taxes?" Nat inquires.

"Fuck! Taxes! I forgot about that. Fucking Uncle Sam! Hmm, maybe I don't want to know." Bekka cries out.

"Doll, it's all good. Forty six percent goes to taxes, but you'll still have plenty left. Trust me, you'll never spend it in this lifetime. Besides, greed is one of the seven deadly sins."

"Yeah, tell that to Uncle Sam!" blurts out Liv.

"We will each walk away with a hefty sum. Forty-one million and forty-one thousand dollars," Nat says excitedly.

"Wow, you're right! We'll never spend it in this lifetime, unless we become spendthrifts. We're rich girls. Really rich!" boasts Bekka.

"Holy shit! It's unbelievable. My mother is going to have a heart attack," Liv states.

"You mean you haven't told her yet?" questions Bekka.

"Well, I spoke to her briefly this morning. I played it off like a normal Sunday morning, as if I was getting the girls ready for religion. I'm going to visit her on Thursday and take her to lunch. I want to give her the news in person. I'm thinking I'll deposit fifty thousand dollars in her account prior to our meeting. It will be just enough proof. Otherwise, she'll never believe it. For me, reality is going to take time to set in. I just can't wait to see her face. I think I'll take a video with my phone," giggles Liv.

"That's such an awesome idea! I love it! It will be a great moment for the two of you. Definitely, tell her in person!" Bekka states.

"Good idea! I think I'll tell my mother and sister the same way. We can watch each other's videos next week. It will be fun!" Nat declares.

"Sounds like there's a knock at the door," Bekka says gazing in Nat's direction.

"It must be lover boy," giggles Liv.

Nat stands up, walks inside, to the wall mirror, giving herself a once over before opening the door. "Hello Phoenix."

"Hi Nat."

"Wow, you clean up nice!"

"Thanks" smiles Pheonix. I can never wait too long to change out of my uniform. It gets a bit itchy when I start perspiring.

"We're hanging on the terrace. Please, join us."

"Good Evening, ladies."

"Hello again, nice to have you back under non-working conditions" laughs Liv.

"Hi Phoenix!" Says Bekka.

"Pop a squat!"

"Interesting choice of words," bursts out Liv.

"Haven't heard that one in a long time."

"Thank you, I think I will. I've been running around all day. The hotel is booked out through the first of the Year."

"Not surprised," adds Nat.

"The pay is pretty consistent so I can't complain. It keeps me afloat between films. The tourists' tip more than celebrities. I can make up to eight hundred dollars a day.

"Wow, that's awesome!" exclaims Nat.

"It's a stimulating place to work. Lots of interesting people and celebrities. Pink was here last week with her daughter Willow. I'm not starstruck, but it is kind of cool to see them trying to live like us."

"Yeah, I bet it is," says Nat.

"By the way, I brought you lovely ladies a few goodies," Phoenix says as he passes Nat a shopping bag.

"Oh, that's so nice and thoughtful of you. Thank you!" Nat says blushing.

"I have a generous employee discount, and I thought you would enjoy some of the delicious sweets from the food hall on the lower level. Don't miss the opportunity to dine there during your stay. The food is very good," says Phoenix confidently.

"Wow! This is too much." Nat shouts out as she places each box one by one on the coffee table. Look girls, all our favorites! Teuscher's, chocolates, cupcakes, meringue cookies, chocolate dipped strawberries, and a bottle of Veuve!"

"So nice! We have not had a chance to dine this visit but, we did enjoy a luncheon here last year. The food is delish. My favorites are from the seafood bar," Liv states.

"I'm going to call our butler and request some ice to chill the bubbly. Thank you again for the goodies. So thoughtful of you," states Bekka as she exits the terrace.

"Yes, very sweet thank you. Hey B, while you're in there please turn up the music" requests Liv.

"Yes Phoenix, very sweet," Nat reiterates.

A moment later the music was jamming and Bekka returned with an ice bucket.

Thirty minutes later the bottle was empty, and they were dancing on the balcony, laughing and enjoying themselves.

"Ladies, let's order another bottle," yelps Liv.

"By the way, I do have one more thing," Phoenix says.

"What's that?" asks Nat as she watches him reach in his pocket.

"A fat doobie," laughs Phoenix.

"That's of course if you want to indulge. No pressure!"

"Of course, we do! It's perfect!" Nat responds with a big smile as she moves her hands to the beat of the music.

"I'll order another bottle. Be right back," says Liv as she shakes her hips through the French doors.

"Why don't we spark this baby up?" proposes Phoenix.

"Go for it!" says Nat.

Bekka takes the first drag. "Wow, this is good shit!" she states, as she takes another hit."

"Well, we wouldn't know it because you're totally hogging it up!" says Nat.

"Yeah, really. Pass that baby this way!" requests Liv as she enters the terrace.

Phoenix looked at the three of them and started laughing.

"What's so funny, lover boy?" Asks Bekka.

"You girls are so funny. Your expressions and remarks are killing me. You're all a lot of fun to be around. I'm glad I met you."

"Well, thank you. That's a compliment coming from a young stud like you," remarks Liv.

"So, tell us, how long have you been acting? Have you done any big films?" Inquires Bekka shaking her hair into the cool breeze.

"Well, I started as a catalog model for Sears when I was seven and that lasted a few years. Then, at age thirteen my agent at the time got me a small part in some of the daytime soaps. All My Children and General Hospital, which I'm sure you're all familiar with."

"Yes, we certainly are," responds Bekka.

"I've had small parts in some major films like Men in Black, The Frockers, American Pie. Currently, I'm auditioning for Girls Night Out 2, as one of the main characters. I've been in the business for twenty-five years. It's tough! It takes a long time to get started in this business but when it takes off it's very exciting."

"Wow, sounds amazing! I wish you the best of luck. Hope you're a big star one day, Phoenix," Nat says in a flirtatious tone as she grabs his hand and starts twirling herself around.

"I can't wait to see Girls Night Out 2," states Bekka.

"Me, too! The first one was so good. We loved it! We couldn't stop laughing. Remember girls?" inquires Liv.

"Yes, it was great!" Nat and Bekka speak simultaneously.

They continue on until the wee hours of the night drinking, laughing, dancing, and indulging in some sweets.

One by one, they eventually pass out. Phoenix spends the night after he realizes he can barely walk.

MANIC MONDAY

Bekka is the first to wake the next morning. As she stretches her arms above her head, she feels a body close to hers that doesn't quite feel like Nat's. She jumps out of bed quickly thinking, oh my, oh my what have I done, as she stares down at Phoenix' half-naked body rolled up in the bed sheet.

"Liv, Liv wake up!" Bekka whispers.

"What is it, B?" Liv asks as she pulls off her eye mask and sits up.

"Look who's in my bed!"

"Oh shit! How did that happen? Where is Nat?"

"Well, that's what I'm trying to figure out."

"Calm down. Don't jump to conclusions. What time is it?" Liv asks as she climbs out of bed.

"Almost eight am."

"Look B, she's over there."

"Where?"

"At the edge of the bed, with you, and Phoenix. See, her hair hanging out of the sheet, over the side of the bed?"

The two of them bust out laughing as they cover their mouths.

"No need to panic! I'm sure you all passed out. We were really drunk."

"I know, but how did we all end up in bed together when there's an enormous chaise lounge on the other side of the room? Did I do something stupid? I won't be able to face him when he wakes. Let's smother him now with a pillow."

"B, maybe you had sex with Nat," giggles Liv. "It probably looks worse than it is. I'm sure it's innocent. Besides, what happens at the Plaza stays at the Plaza!"

"Well, in that case I'll shut up now," Bekka replies softly as she drifts towards the bathroom.

"Good morning ladies," says Phoenix, stretching his arms outward and yawning.

"Ugh, I have such a migraine!" Nat says as she peeps out from under the sheet.

"We're all going to feel pretty shitty today. But it was worth it! What a great time we had!" says Phoenix.

"Yes, it was one of the funnest nights I've had in a long time. Wasn't it, girls?" Liv asks as Bekka exits the bathroom.

"Yes, it was! Just wish I could remember it all," groans Bekka as she rubs her head.

"Why don't we order breakfast, and start the day? You're more than welcome to stay for breakfast, Phoenix," Liv mentions.

"Thanks for the offer, but I need to get home and clean up. I have an audition at noon today."

"Oh, wow! I hope you feel good enough to perform after last night," chuckles Nat.

"No worries. I have so many auditions that I'm an outlier," laughs Phoenix, as he pulls on his shirt and slips his loafers on.

"Hey Nat, do you think we can have dinner one night this week?" poses Phoenix.

"I would love to! Did I give you my number?"

"Yes, like three times last night. See, you even wrote it on the palm of my hand."

"Geez, I can't remember a thing" giggles Nat.

"I'll walk you to the door."

"Well ladies, the pleasure is all mine. Hope we can do this again sometime soon. Enjoy today and get home safe" Phoenix says smiling as he slowly exits the bedroom.

"It was great meeting you," Liv shouts.

"Yes, it was a lot of fun. Good luck with your audition. Looking forward to seeing you on the big screen," replies Bekka.

"Ciao, ladies!"

A few minutes later Nat returns.

"So, what do you think?"

"What do we think? Huh! He's even hotter in the morning with his bedhead!" Bekka blurts out.

"Yes, that is true," agrees Nat.

"I think I need to know how the three of us ended up in the same bed. I know we puffed our brains out, imbibed a ton of alcohol but then, what happened? Tell me please, because I don't recall a thing," Bekka urges.

"B, to tell you the truth, we were just talking and laughing a lot and then we passed out. I can't recall every detail myself, but I know it was fun."

"Yes, it was," Liv chimes in.

"Don't sweat it doll! We have other things to focus on. Today, is an amazing day for the three of us! Our new life and new journey begins! So, let's file it under a fun evening and leave it at that."

"Okay, you're right. I'm over analyzing it. I guess it comes with age. I will order breakfast for us now and then jump in the shower."

"I think he's sweet and he really likes you, Nat. Go to dinner with him" says Liv. "You need to try a new flavor! Don't over think the age thing. He's mature, generous, ambitious and happy. Those rich men you're dating are married, or say they're single, which makes them liars, and even worse!

"They have more baggage than they care to reveal. Who knows what they're really honest about. They think impressing pretty girls gets them laid. You're like an accessory for them. They're actors with big egos as far as I'm concerned, excluding Jacob! Rich jerks that lack genuineness. You have nothing to lose."

"Yes, I totally agree. You're right. It's been one distraction after another. I have to admit I am sick of it. It's like I'm on call for them when they're in town. And quite frankly, I'm bored with all the fancy restaurants, hotels and over-salted decadent meals."

"Well today, is a new beginning. Things are going to be different. It's up to me to make changes. My whole perspective on life in the past twenty-four hours has been altered. I'm going to focus on what really makes me happy and that alone," expresses Nat.

"Well, good then! You know, Bekka and I will support you one hundred percent." KNOCK, KNOCK. Liv stops speaking and rushes to the door. The food has arrived.

Bekka strolls out of the bathroom wearing a navy blue tee, straight-legged jeans, and her hair in a twist. "Perfect timing," she thinks, witnessing the cart moving out to the terrace."

"Well, here's to a perfect weekend ladies," Nat states, raising her glass of fresh squeezed orange juice.

"Yes, and to the future," adds Liv as she takes in the sound of the morning rush hour.

"Yes, to the future," says Bekka.

"Let's make a promise that every year on this day we'll celebrate. No matter what day it falls on. We'll book this room and stay a couple of nights," states Liv.

"Sounds great!" Bekka and Nat agree, "Love it!"

They enjoy breakfast in the morning light, with a spectacular view, and the humming of the city. It was very zen for the three of them.

Nat broke the silence by shouting out "Girls, shall we head out?" in a manic tone.

"Yes!" Liv and Bekka respond.

"Let's go then! Jaxson is waiting out front," informs Liv as they grab their handbags and scatter out the door and into the elevator.

"Bye ladies, thank you for staying with us. Come back soon," says the bellhop holding the elevator door as they pile out.

"Thank you. I have butterflies in my stomach," confesses Nat as they exit the hotel.

"Me too, I was just going to say that," says Bekka.

"It's normal," adds Liv.

"Good Morning, ladies. How are you today?"

"Good Morning, Jaxson," Liv replies.

"We're just great!" says Bekka smiling as she watches herds of people in professional attire bustle down the street.

"Glad to hear it. A good way to start the week!" replies Jaxson.

"Where to, today ladies?"

"Well, first we're going downtown. 15 Beaver Street." The girls remain quiet taking in their life changing reality as the car proceeds around Grand Army Plaza and down Fifth Avenue.

"Holy shit! Oh, my God! Oh, my God!" Yells out Nat with a worried look on her face.

"What is it?" replies Liv.

"We forgot to take the ticket with us. It's in the safe." Nat whispers.

"Oh my! Ok, calm down. Jaxson, we need to head back to the hotel. Immediately please," requests Nat.

"Who put it in the safe in the first place?" asks Bekka.

"I did!" says Liv.

"It was the safest place. I felt it would be too risky and we'd lose it while we were trekking all over town, remember? You both agreed with me."

"No problem, ladies. We'll be there in a few minutes," Jaxson responds enthusiastically.

"Who's going to handle the front desk?" asks Bekka.

"Don't worry, I will. Just relax. I'm sure our room hasn't been cleaned yet."

"I can't help but to think..."

"Shhhhh!" says Liv.

"Please don't think, period!"

Ten minutes later, Liv entered the lobby. Trying not to display how anxious she was, she politely requests entry to the room informing the desk clerk she left something behind. The clerk informs the manager and he obliges immediately, motioning Liv towards the elevator and directly to the suite. He opens the door, lets her in and waits patiently in the hallway.

Olivia opens the safe and couldn't believe her eyes. It was totally bare.

"Holy shit," she thinks as her legs feel as if they are falling out beneath her. She puts her head in her hands, and hyperventilates.

Calm down, calm down. Think Olivia, think she says to herself trying to recall last night's events. She pulls her cell phone out of her bag and sees four texts from Nat. She calls her number trying to stay calm. Nat answers immediately.

"Well, do you have it? Please tell me you have it," screams Nat.

"You're not going to believe this."

"What? Tell me."

"The safe is bare. I'm freaking out. My legs are ready to go out from under me. I feel faint."

"No fucking way! Are you playing a joke on us because this isn't funny!!!"

Liv hears Bekka in the background screaming "Oh my god, oh my god. Kill me now!"

"Tell Bekka to shut up and stop making things worse. I'm tearing the place apart and I suggest the two of you come up and join me."

"We'll be right up!" Nat says frantically.

Liv continues searching high and low, looking under the beds, between the sheets and in the garbage pails. She looks everywhere possible. Sweat starts beading down her forehead.

Nat & Bekka enter the room like they're on fire. Nat is screaming and Bekka is crying.

"What the fuck? How the fuck could this happen? Nat, did you tell your lover boy about it?" accuses Bekka.

"No, I absolutely did not tell him!" she shouts out.

"I did not tell him anything. What do you think, I'm crazy?!"

"Well, you tend to have loose lips when you're drunk," Bekka says as she squints at Nat.

"Really! You know B, you're such a bitch! Ain't my fault!" yells Nat.

"Enough! Just stop it! I feel like I'm with my kids now. They fight over petty nonsense. It's not going to change anything!" Liv interjects.

"But this isn't nonsense!" says Bekka.

"Let's just sit down, take a breath and think. You know the saying, what you're looking for is usually right in front of you" Liv states.

"I recall the first night we checked in and I put the ticket in the safe. I gave the two of you the code in case you wanted to put some valuables in there. I haven't opened it since. So, did either of you open it? Nat, I recall you saying you were putting your chandelier earrings in there," inquires Liv.

"Yes, and I did do that."

"I didn't go near the safe once," Bekka chimes in.

"So, where are the earrings? Did you take them out?"

"Hmm, good question. I can't quite remember."

"Well, you're not wearing them. So where could they be?" Liv asks, waiting patiently for Nat's response.

"I'm not sure. I am so panicked right now I can't think straight."

"Why don't you check your handbag? It's possible you don't remember putting them in there, and maybe the ticket, too."

Nat stood up and walked briskly over to the entryway table and grabbed her bag. When she returns, she dumps the contents on the bed and starts sifting through it nervously. She opens her mini-makeup bag, finds a lip gloss, mirror, hair tie and mints. As she unzips the inner pockets, she starts to recall putting her earrings in there.

"Well, here are the earrings. We're getting warmer girls," Nat says feeling calmer.

Bekka and Liv continue searching the room moving in opposite directions until they hear Nat scream out, "Ah haaaa!"

Liv and Bekka run into the bedroom to find Nat holding up the lottery ticket screaming "I found it! I found it! Thank God, I found it!"

She jumps on Liv and Bekka, throws her arms up and hugs them tightly.

"Oh, thank you god!" yells out Bekka "I apologize for getting bitchy Nat. I definitely got a few grey hairs in the last fifteen minutes."

"And I grew a mustache," giggles Liv.

"Apology accepted" says Nat.

"Where the fuck was it?"

"Neatly tucked away in my wallet. I obviously forgot I put it there. Now, we'll appreciate it more than ever," Nat says as she kisses it.

"Let's go! It's after ten. I'll hold the ticket" insists Liv.

They exit the hotel and head straight to the car. Jaxson can tell from their expressions that everything was okay.

"We're back!" states Liv.

"Thanks for your patience," adds Nat.

"No problem. It's part of the job. Are we still heading to 15 Beaver Street ladies?"

"Yes, we sure are! Thanks Jaxson".

"You got it, ladies!"

"Wow girls. How frigging crazy was that?" Liv says with a sigh of relief.

"Totally cray-cray. I'm glad it's over!" exhales Bekka. "Now, onto bigger and better things."

"Yes, so excited!" squeals Nat.

"Let's just relax, girls. We're almost there," says Liv as she puts her hand on her chest. "My heart finally stopped racing."

"I don't think mine is going to stop," adds Nat.

"Ladies, here we are, at your request."

"My heart is racing," says Bekka.

"Mine is starting up again. I'm getting such a rush," says Liv.

"I'll wait for you here ladies."

"Thanks Jaxon," Liv says as she exits the SUV.

They walk into the lobby silently as if walking into a mass. They spot the directory and walk over to it.

"Here we go!" Natalia points to the big bold letters NEW YORK LOTTERY CUSTOMER SERVICE CENTERS second floor.

"Second floor, girls. We all have our ID, right?"

"Yes, we have what we need. No more drama," confirms Bekka.

They rode the elevator with a handful of people, not saying a word. They made eye contact with each other and revealed a hint of a smile knowing that this moment was going to change their lives forever.

"So, ladies, you want it all in one lump sum?" asks the clerk behind the glass window.

"Yes, but divided equally in thirds please," requests Liv.

"I think this is the best way to avoid worrying that the tax rate may increase over time. Let's just get it all out of the way," Nat whispers.

"I need to see your ID's and you each need to fill out individual tax forms. There are pens at the opposite counter if you need them."

"Okay, thank you" Liv says, handing the clerk the ID's with a shaky hand.

"Here are the forms. Take your time, ladies. When you're finished just walk back to my window and hand them to me. It takes about fifteen minutes for us to verify everything and cut the check."

Nat's hand begins to shake as she signs her name. Liv's feeling hot and anxious. Bekka starts complaining that the form is too long, and they ask for too much information.

"Shhh, just shut up and fill it out! Most women would give their left tit to be in this situation. We'll be walking out of here in no time as three rich princesses" Liv states.

"Okay, here you are," Nat says to the clerk handing over the docs.

"Ladies have a seat. We'll call you shortly," states the clerk.

"I'm running to the bathroom. I'm so nervous" confesses Liv.

"Me, too. I'll join you." Nat follows Liv into the bathroom.

"Then, I guess we'll all go. It will kill some time. I feel so parched," says Bekka.

"What a crappy bathroom. It's a smelly mess. I feel nausea," says Nat.

"What did you expect marble tiles and a jacuzzi?" Bekka rebuts turning sideways in front of the mirror to see if she's bloated from the weekend's indulgences.

"Who cares about the bathroom! We'll be out of here in fifteen minutes, forever!" Liv adds.

"Are we ready now?" asks Nat.

Bekka and Liv nod in agreement. Just as they appear in the waiting area, they hear the clerk yell out, "Ladies, we're ready for you."

"Jesus, my heart is definitely racing now," Liv says.

"Mine, too. I feel faint," says Nat.

"Don't get so dramatic. Pretend you're high. Like you were in high school," Bekka replies.

The clerk continues. "Okay, ladies, after tax, the total is one hundred twenty-three million, one hundred and twenty thousand. Divided by three, gives each of you forty-one million and forty thousand dollars. Don't spend it all in one place. Here are your ID's, a copy of your tax form, your checks and a list of ten things "To-Do" when you hit the lottery. Congratulations!"

"This is amazing! Wow, thank you, thank you, so much!." Liv says as she grabs everything, and turns to Bekka and Nat with watery eyes.

They share a group hug. Tears run down their cheeks.

"Let's take a selfie, girls. We'll definitely look back at this moment years from now," insists Nat.

"Yes, that's for sure," agrees Bekka.

With big smiles, they hold up their checks and squeeze together to take a few selfies before heading to the elevator.

"Hello. Hello, earth to Nat. Hit G for ground floor," Bekka says.

"Sorry, I just spaced out thinking about the amount of the check. I've never seen one with so many zeros in my life," says Nat as she presses the button.

"It's amazing that they actually give you a to-do list. Maybe they should be handing out a not-to-do-list!"

They all laugh.

"It is funny," adds Liv.

"Hi ladies. Where to?" asks Jaxson as they pile into the car.

"Good question," Liv turns to Bekka and Nat with a big smile across her face.

"Well, I think I'll take your advice Liv and take the day off," says Nat.

"I'll just go home and hang. After all, I do need to call my mother and sister and fill them in. Maybe, I'll even call Phoenix," she giggles.

"Jaxson, fifty-second and second please.

I'll stop at the bank first and walk home from there. I could really use some fresh air," exhales Nat.

"Yes, that's the right thing to do. Plus, you need to digest the whole experience. We all do! It's going to take some time. We need to make a plan," says Liv.

"Jaxon we'll be heading to Brooklyn once we drop Nat off," Bekka chimes in.

"Sure thing, ladies."

"Thank you, Jaxon."

"Look at this list. It's quite interesting" whispers Liv.

Ten Things "To-Do" When You Hit The Lottery

They look over the list together. As Jaxson continues to drive, Liv reads off the list softly, line by line.

"1. Remain anonymous if your state rules permit it.

2. See a tax pro before you cash the ticket.

3. Avoid sudden lifestyle changes.

4. Pay off all your debts.

5. Assemble a team of legal and financial advisers.

6. Invest prudently.

7. Live within a budget."

"Oh well, it's too late for number two and number seven" giggles Bekka enamored with her winnings.

"Going forward girls, we must discipline ourselves and be mindful," says Nat.

"Yes, for sure," Liv confirms as she continues to read the list.

"8. Take steps to protect assets.

9. Plan charitable gifts.

10. Review your estate plan."

"Well, these are certainly some helpful guidelines to consider. Definitely hang on to it!" Liv suggests as she folds her copy and places it in her handbag.

"Well, here we are ladies, fifty-second and second at your request," reports Jaxson.

"Thank you so much! Hope to see you soon, Jaxson. Take care," says Nat in an excited tone.

Liv and Bekka jump out of the car to say goodbye.

"Let's talk later on. I love you," says Liv.

"Love you, too."

"Yes, let's check in with each other once the dust settles. I love you," says Bekka.

"Love you more. You need to pinch me. This is just amazing!" laughs Nat.

"Bye, bye girlfriends" she says as she takes a few strides forward, pivots and looks back. She waves, blows a kiss in the air, and disappears into the crowd.

"So, where to?" asks Jaxson.

"To Brooklyn please. Bay Ridge. Thank you," says Liv.

"You got it."

Bekka pulls out pictures of her kids from her wallet. She smiles.

"I miss mine so much my heart aches. I can't wait to see them!" says Liv.

"I need to do one thing before I go home."

"What's that?" asks Liv.

"You'll see."

"Jaxson, can you drop me off on ninetieth and Fifth Avenue, please?"

"Sure thing."

"Ninetieth and fifth? What's there? I can't think of anything other than my old vet."

"Are you getting the kids a puppy?"

"No. I'm doing something I've been wanting to do for a long time and now I know why it didn't happen sooner."

"Why?" Liv asks.

"Because, now I can do it on my own and nothing feels better than that."

"Curiosity is killing me. Give me a hint."

"It's shiny."

"Hmm, shiny? I am clueless."

"You'll know soon enough."

"Okay, then, ninetieth and fifth, it is!" Liv insists as they enjoy the ride into Brooklyn reminiscing about the weekend.

"Jaxson, you can let me off in the middle of the next block."

"You got it!" he replies as the vehicle moves past the green light.

Liv continues to stare out the window until the vehicle comes to a stop in front of the Mercedes dealership.

"Right here is perfect!"

"Ha ha ha, now I get it!" says Liv. "I'm so happy for you. Are you actually doing it?"

"Yes, I am! A silver S550 with all the bells and whistles. Then, I promise to behave for a while. Just a little while," says Bekka with a mischievous wink.

"Yeah, right! Like you said, they should have handed us a *not-to-do list*," giggles Liv.

"Do you want me to come with you?"

"No. Go home to your girls. I'm sure they're dying to see you. I'll swing by your house to show off my new wheels," smiles Bekka.

"Sounds good. Have fun, Bekka! Relish the moment."

"Oh, I will. Love you and speak to you later," Bekka says as she hugs Liv.

"Love you too" and the car door shuts. Liv observes Bekka for a few seconds strutting towards the dealership with a big smile and her hair blowing in the wind, as the car pulls away. Liv imagines Bekka will drive the salesperson crazy.

"This is our bar, Jaxon," Liv points out as the car whizzes by Bar Divine. "That's where we started this weekend."

"Looks like a cool place," Jaxson replies.

"You live in a nice neighborhood."

Liv feels butterflies in her stomach as she turns to look at the deli where they bought the ticket. Who would have guessed it would turn out like this, as she feels herself getting goosebumps.

"Make the next right and then the first right. My house is on the right side in the middle of the block. The beige home with the white porch."

"What a pretty neighborhood, Liv. You must love it here. It's so close to the city too."

"Yes, we do love it. My girls too. You can pull up behind the white van."

"You got it!"

"Here you go. I hope I'll hear from you ladies again. The pleasure has been all mine."

"Absolutely! We'll be in the back seat of your car before you know it! Thank you so much Jaxon. You've been amazing!"

Liv slides out of the car, shakes Jaxson's hand and says goodbye. She walks up to the front porch and feels happy she's finally home.

WHATEVER AFTER

Liv wonders what the girls are up to. She wants to surprise them. She slides her key in the door, pauses and presses her ear against it and listens. She hears the dogs running around and the television. She turns around, to enjoy the beautiful fall colors, and the light breeze, before easing back into reality.

She sits on the porch, something she hasn't done in a long time. Liv observes and listens to everything around her. She tries to stay in the moment, but her attention is drawn to a school bus shuttling down the street. The kids are screaming, and their heads and arms are dangling out the windows. She looks across the street. Her neighbor is unloading groceries out of her car.

The birds are chirping. The fall colors are vibrant. The scent of fall is intoxicating. She takes it all in, enjoying moments of solidarity and reflects back on her life. Liv couldn't help but to think this could not have come at a better time. Her hardships, successes, and her life's journey prepared her. Struggling was her norm, so much of her past was still hard to shake. She won't allow the money to change who she is.

It took this long to become who I am. To like myself! I promise to keep things in perspective, be responsible. Maybe I'll pretend it never happened, pay off the mortgage, fix up a few things around the house and leave it at that. And when the girls go off to college, I'll pretend I received an inheritance to pay for it. I will donate to a charity and start a foundation to raise money for human oocyte cryopreservation for women who can't afford it.

Liv laughs at her thoughts. There, my mind goes again. It won't stop. I can't be left alone. I need distraction. I'm becoming paranoid. I don't want to feel like a different person next week. I want to recognize myself! Money can make people crazy. It's known to be the root of all evil. Evil spelled backwards is live.

BEEP. BEEP.

Suddenly, her thoughts are interrupted by the sound of a horn and the tempo of a fast car which comes to a full stop in front of her driveway. She hears someone calling her name.

Liv stands up, smiles, and walks to the stairs.

"What do you think?" Bekka shouts as she waves her hands out of a convertible.

"It's so beautiful and you look amazing in it!" Liv replies excitedly giving Bekka a thumbs up and blows her a kiss as she pulls away.

Still smiling, Liv walks toward the front door and puts her key in. This is it, she thinks. I'm ready! A new chapter of my life begins. Right now!

"Girls, girls, mommy's home!"

EPILOGUE

Olivia (4 weeks later)

Next stop, Cortlandt Street. A homeless guy slogs by like a snail. It smells like he shit in his pants. He shakes a styrofoam cup with a few coins. He leaves a stench behind that could char your nostril hairs. DING! The subway doors close.

This is it! Olivia closes her Real Estate exam prep book. Feeling confident, she carefully slides it into her backpack, zips it up and slides her arms through the straps. She stands up, gracefully maintaining her balance as the car comes to a screeching halt.

The doors fly open. Olivia wants to call Jack to let him know she is at the testing site and to remind him that he's picking up the girls. She withdraws her cell phone from her windbreaker, and dials, as she exits the subway stairwell.

"Hi, I just got off the train."

"Hey!"

"Jack, today is the day I take my exam. I'm a couple of blocks away from the building. I'm just calling to remind you to pick the girls up from school."

"Yes, Liv, don't worry. I'll drop them off by 5pm. Good luck!"

"It should be easy-peasy. Thank you."

"Gotta go. Bye, Liv!"

"Bye!"

Olivia enters 123 William Street and takes the elevator to the second floor. "ID please," the test administrator requests. Olivia retrieves her id from her wallet.

"Thank you. Now please sign in. Take a pencil if you need one and find a seat. The test will start in fifteen minutes. No food or drink is permitted in this room. The restrooms are down the hall on the right."

"Okay, thank you." Olivia scans the room and chooses the first desk in the center row and sits. She places her backpack down, removes her jacket and drapes it over the back of the chair. She takes a deep breath and then exhales as she observes faces around her.

"I wonder what inspired them to get into real estate?" she thinks. Such a diverse mix of people, from all walks of life, all brought together for the common interest of obtaining the freedom to be their own boss. How many of us will actually be successful? If we are, do we have to be like sharks in a tank? Suddenly, Olivia's thoughts were broken by laughter and chatter coming from two females behind her.

"Yeah Dez! We need to go ouuuut this weeeeekend.! Me, you and Gina need to hit the town. Thank god we won't be sittin' in that smelly, boring-ass classroom anymore. In ninety minutes, this nonsense will be over. We need to go out and celebrate. And I say we buy a lottery ticket. We each pick some numbers like those pretty white chicks from Brooklyn.

"Look what happened to them. They won two hundred, and twenty-eight million dollars. Imagine a girls' night out, a few drinks and a lottery ticket. Two hundred and twenty-eight million lucky! It's in the newspaper, and everything.

"They're not only rich, they're famous too. They donated a million dollars to Kids with Cancer Research Foundation. They are some good-hearted white chicks. Now, I say we try our luck at that. Wha'd you say D?"

"I say we go for it, Keisha. They ain't any better than us. We could get lucky too, ya know. I don't wanna start looking for a job until after the holidays anyway. Dwayne can keep paying my expenses until I get in with a good brokerage. And, if we hit lotto, I'm dumping his big ass and replacing it with some custom Louie Vuitton bags, Louboutin shoes, diamond studs and a Mercedes coupe."

Olivia giggled silently as she stretched her arms above her head trying to get comfortable in the hardback chair.

The testing monitor entered the room. "Okay, ladies and gentlemen, please put all your books away and turn your phones off. We're going to distribute the test now. You can start as soon as it hits your desk. Test time ends at exactly three thirty and there will be no excuses. You've all had plenty of time to prepare for today. Are there any questions?"

The room went dead silent. Olivia started the test as soon as it landed in front of her. She was ready to be a real estate agent.

Liv arrives home and calls out to the girls, "Hi Loves! Mommy's home."

"Hey Mom."

Liv walks into the den and glances around to see if Jack is hanging around.

"Dad just dropped us off a few minutes ago."

"How did it go Mama?" Bea asks.

"Yeah Mom, how did you do?" Nikki yells out.

"Tell us. Was it easy?" Juliet chimes in.

Liv reveals a big smile as she looks at her daughters.

"Mommy aced it!" she shouts out.

ACKNOWLEDGEMENTS

Jessica Hester consultant, editor, sister from a past life and dear friend. I thank you for your amazing insight, patience and creativity.

Jessica is a filmmaker and started her career in theatre.

https://www.imdb.com/name/nm3911822/

Ibnul Affan P is an illustrator from Indonesia. He designed the book cover for my debut novel which exceeded my expectations. He is an experienced graphic designer. His illustration designs are intense with rich colors, detail and characters. The result is a honed experience and masterpiece at its best. Never underestimate the talented people on Fiverr!

https://www.fiverr.com/ibnulaffan

To my mother Josephine
Without you I would not exist. Thank you for all your love, care and perseverance. I love you to the moon and back!

Nadia, Bella & Julianna The three loves of my life. You took me on a journey that I could have never dreamed of. I am so proud to be your mother. You're everything I imagined to be and more.

To my girlfriends Thank you for being amazing women and for all the laughs and tears, we share. We are connected no matter how often, or seldom we see each other. Time is the only distance between us. Ti amo!

To my readers I hope you will enjoy Girls Night Out, and I thank you for taking the time to read it. Follow us on Instagram **@gno_girlsnightout**